The Monarch Legacy

Truth may sleep, but it dreams of being found

Tumblebrook Mysteries
Book 2

Ellen Le Teace

Chapter 1

A Vanishing Welcome

The early morning mist clung to the eaves of the Tumblebrook Inn as Amelia Farnsworth smoothed the front of her crisp linen apron. She had spent the past hour ensuring the parlor was flawless—bookshelves freshly dusted, a fire crackling in the hearth, and the warm scent of cinnamon scones drifting from the kitchen. Everything had to be perfect. Today was a special day.

Tobias Greer, the esteemed travel writer, was set to arrive.

Amelia had read his columns for years, marveling at how he captured the soul of tucked-away towns with words that danced. His praise was transformative—places featured in his articles saw a surge of tourism, attention, and acclaim. Now, Tumblebrook was under his discerning gaze. If his visit went well, the inn might be featured in his next piece.

A soft trill interrupted her thoughts. Lady Grey, her sleek British Shorthair, sat poised near the bay window, her intelligent amber eyes fixed on the approaching figure outside.

"You always know when someone's coming, don't you?" Amelia mused, scratching the cat gently behind the ears.

Lady Grey flicked her tail but didn't break her gaze. A moment later, the heavy oak door swung inward with a reluctant sigh, and Tobias Greer stepped inside.

"Mr. Greer! Welcome to Tumblebrook Inn," Amelia greeted warmly, offering her most practiced and genuine smile.

Tobias removed his hat, shaking a few stray raindrops from his thick, graying hair. His sharp eyes swept the room, absorbing the cozy charm with the quiet discernment of a seasoned traveler. Dressed in a tailored overcoat and carrying a well-worn leather satchel, he exuded an air of quiet authority.

"Thank you, Ms. Farnsworth," he said, offering a firm handshake. His voice was deep, cultured, carrying the weight of a man who had seen the world and written about it.

"Please, call me Amelia."

He gave a curt nod before glancing down. Lady Grey had slinked forward, weaving through his legs before stopping cold. Her ears flattened slightly, and her whiskers twitched. Instead of her usual friendly purr, she merely observed him in eerie silence.

Tobias arched a brow. "Your cat has an interesting way of greeting guests."

"She's usually quite the charmer," Amelia admitted, puzzled by Lady Grey's sudden hesitance. "Perhaps she's just being shy."

"Hm." Tobias didn't seem convinced, but he moved on, adjusting his satchel. "I trust my room is ready?"

"Of course. Right this way."

As Amelia led him up the grand staircase, Lady Grey lingered behind, her tail flicking as she watched them disappear down the hall.

By the time Amelia set out the afternoon tea, the rain had thickened into a steady curtain. Tobias had requested solitude after settling into his room, which wasn't uncommon—some guests preferred privacy to rest after traveling. Still, something about his behavior felt... off.

Just as the grandfather clock chimed four, Tobias re-emerged.

The parlor filled with the scent of bergamot as Amelia poured steaming tea into delicate porcelain cups. A floral-patterned tray held finger sandwiches, fresh scones, and golden shortbread.

"Tea?" Amelia offered, setting out the china with her usual care.

Tobias accepted with a nod, his gaze distracted as he stirred his tea absently. His small leather journal rested on the table beside him —open, but unread.

"I hope you've found the inn to your liking so far?" she asked, trying not to sound too eager.

"Yes. It's... charming."

Not exactly the enthusiastic praise she'd hoped for.

Amelia watched as he broke a scone in half but didn't eat it. He glanced at the fire, then at his journal, and finally at the window.

"You must travel quite a bit for your writing."

"Yes," he said simply, then paused. "I prefer places with history. Towns with secrets."

Something in his voice made Amelia glance at him sharply. His tone was neutral, but his eyes weren't.

"Well, Tumblebrook has plenty of both," she offered, smiling thinly.

"More than most," he murmured.

Lady Grey, who had been perched on the windowsill, suddenly let out a low, guttural sound. Tobias stiffened.

"She doesn't seem to like me," he muttered.

"She's particular about people," Amelia replied, though Lady Grey's unease mirrored her own.

Tobias exhaled and closed his journal. "I think I'll turn in early. Tomorrow will be a long day."

"Of course. Let me know if you need anything."

That night, a thunderstorm rolled through the valley, shaking the shutters and whistling through the chimney. Amelia tossed under the covers, her mind replaying Tobias's words. Towns with secrets. More than most.

She couldn't shake the feeling that he'd meant more than just history.

A loud creak in the hallway startled her. She sat upright. Silence.

Lady Grey jumped down from the windowsill, tail high and alert. A low growl rumbled from her throat.

Amelia wrapped herself in a robe and crept into the hall. The inn was quiet. But the hairs on the back of her neck stood up.

She descended the stairs slowly. The fire had died down, casting flickering shadows. Outside, lightning flashed.

Then—movement near the front door.

Amelia froze.

Lady Grey darted ahead, stopping abruptly. Her body tensed.

Amelia inched toward the door and pulled it open.

Nothing. Just wind and rain.

But then she saw it: a partial footprint in the mud—large, booted, and fresh.

She locked the door quickly, heart pounding. Lady Grey meowed sharply, circling her feet.

The next morning, light filtered through lace curtains. The storm had passed.

Amelia dressed and went downstairs, expecting to find Tobias with his tea.

Instead, the dining room was empty.

The teacup from the night before still sat on the parlor table, untouched.

Amelia knocked on Tobias's door. No answer.

She opened it. The bed was untouched. His coat still hung on the chair. His bag was packed.

"Mr. Greer?"

Nothing.

She stepped back, unsettled.

Lady Grey leapt onto the windowsill, eyes narrowed.

Amelia followed her gaze. There was no one outside.

Then she noticed something on the floor—just beyond her door.

A folded note.

She unfolded the note.

He knows too much.

Her pulse thundered.

Lady Grey hissed softly.

Amelia backed away from the window.

Tobias Greer had vanished.

And someone in Tumblebrook didn't want him found.

Chapter 2

A Mysterious Aura

Morning light streamed through the lace curtains of the Tumblebrook Inn, casting soft golden patches on the wooden floor. Amelia Farnsworth stood in the dining room, gazing at the place setting meant for Tobias Greer. The uneaten breakfast—a plate of fluffy scrambled eggs and crisp bacon—sat cooling on delicate porcelain. The tea she had brewed for him had already gone tepid.

A traveler leaving in the middle of the night wasn't unheard of, but Tobias hadn't packed, hadn't checked out—hadn't even left a note. No, something was wrong. A knot of unease twisted in her stomach, and she knew she wouldn't be able to rest until she had answers.

She picked up the fine china cup and dumped the tea into the sink, her brow furrowed. If Tobias had left willingly, where had he gone? More importantly, why?

Lady Grey, as if sensing her unease, padded into the kitchen and let out a soft meow. The sleek British Shorthair had been acting strangely since Tobias's arrival, and this morning was no different.

She weaved between Amelia's legs before darting out and up the stairs.

"Lady Grey?" Amelia called, drying her hands on a towel before following her.

At the top of the staircase, she found Lady Grey seated directly in front of Tobias's door, tail twitching.

"You're still curious about his room, aren't you?" Amelia murmured, placing her hands on her hips.

The cat flicked her ears and pawed at the base of the door.

Amelia hesitated. Entering a guest's room uninvited wasn't exactly ideal—but given the circumstances, she could justify it. Taking a breath, she turned the brass doorknob and stepped inside.

The room was just as Tobias had left it. His suitcase lay open, filled with neatly folded clothes. The leather journal he'd been scribbling in during tea rested on the desk. The bed remained untouched, its covers smooth and undisturbed.

A chill passed through her. If he had left of his own accord, he would have taken his things.

Lady Grey hopped onto the bed, sniffing the pillows before leaping down and prowling toward the nightstand. Her tail twitched again as she lowered her nose to the floor and let out a small chirp.

"What is it?" Amelia knelt beside her, running her fingers along the floorboards. Something glinted faintly under the bedframe.

With care, she reached underneath and retrieved a small, crumpled scrap of paper. Its edges were torn. Frowning, she unfolded it.

The paper held a series of strange symbols—delicate, looping, unfamiliar.

A shiver crept down her spine.

Lady Grey let out a soft sound, nudging her hand.

"I think we need help," Amelia whispered, rising to her feet.

There was only one person in Tumblebrook who might understand: Clara Henderson.

* * *

The bookstore, Gossamer Fables, sat at the heart of Tumblebrook's main street. Its bay windows displayed old tomes, bestsellers, and whimsical trinkets. Normally, Amelia found the scent of parchment and coffee comforting. Today, she was here with purpose.

A brass bell chimed as she pushed open the door. Behind the counter, Clara Henderson looked up from her stack of books.

Clara had been one of Amelia's closest friends since she'd arrived in Tumblebrook. A native, Clara had grown up with her nose in books while other kids played tag. Her love of logic puzzles and history made her a scholar at heart, and her job as a clerk at Gossamer Fables—and part-time cook at the inn—was the perfect fit.

"To what do I owe the pleasure?" Clara asked, pushing up her glasses.

"I need your help," Amelia said. "It's Tobias Greer. He's missing."

Clara's smile faded. "Missing?"

Amelia nodded. "He never checked out, but he's gone. His suitcase is still there. I found this under his bed." She handed Clara the scrap of paper.

Clara examined it, her lips pressed tight. "These symbols... they're unusual. I'll check the archives."

She stepped behind the rolling ladder and retrieved a heavy tome. "This one's on cryptic scripts—merchant codes, scholar markings..."

As she flipped pages, her finger paused on a section filled with ornate symbols. "Tumblebrook has a long history of hidden messages. Smugglers once used markings on stones and trees to signal safe paths."

Amelia leaned in. "Could this be connected?"

"Possibly. Tobias might've stumbled onto something."

"He said something odd during tea—about towns with secrets. That Tumblebrook had more than most."

Clara glanced up. "That's not small talk."

"No. And Lady Grey's been on edge since he got here."

"I'll keep this quiet," Clara said. "But if something's going on—"

"We need to know what it is," Amelia agreed.

* * *

Back at the inn, Amelia and Clara sat at the dining table. The paper lay between them. Lady Grey perched nearby, eyes fixed on it.

Clara flipped through books filled with ciphers and code.

"None of these match exactly," she said. "They're too stylized. Could be a cipher—or a personal language."

Amelia stared at the paper. "Maybe his journal has clues."

They returned to Tobias's room. Amelia picked up the journal and opened to the last page.

A phrase was scrawled in hurried ink:

The key is hidden where the water meets the stone.

Clara looked at her. "What does that mean?"

"I don't know," Amelia replied. "But I think we're about to find out."

Lady Grey let out a soft chirp, as if to say, finally.

And deep in Amelia's gut, she knew—they were just getting started.

Chapter 3

Seeking Clara's Insight

Clara Henderson had always possessed an inquisitive mind. It was what had drawn her to books, puzzles, and eventually the quiet thrill of research. Now, as she sat in the parlor of Tumblebrook Inn with morning sunlight spilling across the table, she studied the strange scrap of paper Amelia had placed before her. The symbols looped and curled almost decoratively, yet something about them felt deliberate.

The air carried the faint aroma of freshly brewed coffee and warm pastries, remnants of breakfast service still lingering. Lady Grey was curled on the windowsill, her amber eyes fixed on the two women with unblinking curiosity. The inn's wooden beams creaked softly overhead, and from the kitchen came the occasional clink of dishes. Outside, the town stirred to life—the hum of conversation and the distant ring of a bicycle bell drifted through the slightly open window.

It all seemed ordinary. And yet, for the first time in ages, Amelia felt anything but.

Clara adjusted her glasses, leaning in. "It's not an alphabet I recognize," she murmured. "But it's not random, either. It's some kind of cipher."

Amelia, cradling a steaming cup of coffee, watched her closely. "Do you think Tobias was hiding something? Or did he uncover something someone else wanted to stay hidden?"

Clara tapped the table. "Given his profession, it's possible. He didn't just document locations—he uncovered stories. If he found something here, it might've been significant enough to make someone nervous."

Amelia nodded slowly. "He didn't say much. Always scribbling in that journal of his, but careful. Guarded."

"Do you still have the journal?" Clara asked.

Amelia retrieved it from the sideboard and placed it on the table. The leather cover was worn, its pages filled with Tobias's compact, meticulous handwriting.

Clara flipped through, scanning his observations. Notes about the inn. The landscape. The townsfolk. Then, toward the end, a shift in tone.

"Listen to this," she said. "Tumblebrook is a place of many layers. Beneath its idyllic charm lies a history not often spoken of. I feel as though I am close to uncovering something significant—something worth remembering."

A chill settled between them.

"What do you think he meant?" Amelia asked quietly.

Clara's brows furrowed. "It sounds like he found something deeper than local history. Maybe something controversial. Or dangerous."

Amelia wrapped her hands around her cup, trying to shake the unease. "If that's true—and now he's missing—then whatever he found might've been the reason."

Clara studied the cryptic scrap again. "It's a clue. It has to be."

Amelia followed Lady Grey's gaze to the window. "We need answers. Doris Finch might be a good place to start. If anyone's heard something, it's her."

* * *

The Tumblebrook Café sat at the crossroads of town, its checkered curtains and flower-filled windows welcoming early risers with warmth and comfort. Inside, the scent of fresh coffee and baked goods wrapped around patrons like a cozy quilt. It was the kind of place where gossip spread faster than jam on toast.

Doris Finch stood behind the counter, her apron dusted with flour, her eyes sharp with curiosity. As Amelia and Clara entered, she looked up and smirked.

"Well, well. My favorite sleuths," she quipped, drying her hands. "You two look like you've got a question or ten."

Clara stepped forward. "We're looking into Tobias Greer's disappearance."

Doris's eyebrows shot up. "The travel writer? Knew there was something off about him."

"You did?" Amelia asked.

"He asked too many questions. Not just about the town—about the lake, old families, things most people leave alone."

Clara's pulse quickened. "Did he ever mention why?"

"No, but he wasn't alone. I saw him meet someone."

"Who?" Amelia leaned in.

Doris lowered her voice. "A stranger. Tall, well-dressed. Deliberate. Like someone trying to blend in but not quite pulling it off. They met at the corner table."

Clara turned toward the table, now occupied by two elderly men. "When?"

"The evening before Tobias vanished."

Amelia frowned. "And the stranger?"

"Stayed a bit longer. Finished their coffee. Left quietly. Never saw them again."

Clara's thoughts spiraled. Whoever the stranger was, they were the last person known to speak with Tobias. A helper—or a threat?

They ordered tea and scones and took a seat.

Doris, not one to resist a mystery, returned with fresh coffee and more insights. "He was poking around places best left buried. This town's got its stories—buried treasure, family feuds, missing letters. Pick one."

"Do you think someone stopped him?" Clara asked.

Doris sipped her coffee, her tone thoughtful. "If he got close to something... maybe. History has a way of repeating itself."

Clara and Amelia sat back, absorbing it all. If Tobias had uncovered something buried in Tumblebrook's past, it might not have stayed buried for long.

And perhaps someone had gone to great lengths to keep it that way.

Chapter 4

Trails From the Past

The morning air in Tumblebrook carried the crisp bite of early fall, the scent of damp earth mingling with the faint aroma of baked goods drifting from Doris Finch's café. The streets were quiet as Amelia Farnsworth and Clara Henderson made their way to the edge of town, toward the secluded cottage of Ezra, the town's reclusive historian.

Ezra's home sat beyond a winding dirt path, partially obscured by thick trees and tangled underbrush. The cabin, a modest structure of weathered wood and moss-covered stone, looked like something out of a forgotten folktale—complete with a crooked iron gate that creaked as Amelia pushed it open. Wild vines clung to the walls, and bird feeders dangled from tree branches, attracting finches that chirped indignantly at the disturbance.

Lady Grey, who had insisted on accompanying them, wove between Amelia's ankles as they approached the porch. Her ears twitched at every rustle, her tail flicking like a metronome. Clara rapped on the door, the knock sharp against the stillness.

After a pause, the door creaked open just enough for a pair of sharp gray eyes to peer out.

"Well, if it isn't the two most persistent women in Tumblebrook," Ezra rasped, his voice equal parts amusement and suspicion.

"We need your help," Amelia said before he could retreat. "It's about Tobias Greer."

Ezra sighed but stepped aside, gesturing them inside.

The interior of the cabin was a cluttered sanctuary of ink and parchment. Stacks of books, rolled maps, and brittle newspapers filled every available surface. Dust motes floated in the filtered light, and the air smelled of aged paper and pipe smoke. Maps lined the walls, some yellowed with age, their corners curling like leaves in autumn. A large oak desk dominated the far end, buried under notebooks, ink bottles, and magnifying lenses.

Despite his hermit-like lifestyle, Ezra hadn't always lived in seclusion. Decades ago, he had been a respected academic, known for asking inconvenient questions about Tumblebrook's carefully curated history. His deep dives into the town's secretive past—particularly surrounding the elusive Monarch Society—had earned him admiration from a few and wariness from most. When he refused to back down, he was quietly ostracized. Now, he preferred the company of forgotten documents to living townsfolk.

"Make yourselves comfortable," Ezra muttered, settling into a high-backed chair. "What's this about?"

Amelia perched on the edge of an armchair, Lady Grey curled in her lap. "Tobias Greer has gone missing. He was staying at the inn. His belongings are still there. He didn't check out."

Ezra raised an eyebrow. "You think the past made him vanish?"

"He came to see you, didn't he?" Clara asked, already scanning the cluttered room.

Ezra exhaled and reached for a thick notebook. "Yes. A few days ago. He was asking about land records, defunct businesses, and," he paused, "Monarch folklore."

Clara and Amelia exchanged a glance. "He mentioned Monarch by name?" Amelia asked.

Ezra nodded. "He wasn't subtle. Wanted to know if the society still existed. If it ever did. The stories say they influenced land deals, elections, even business ownership. Tumblebrook's most powerful families were rumored to be involved."

"And what do you believe?" Clara asked.

Ezra's expression darkened. "Too many missing records. Too many unexplained land transfers. People vanishing without questions. It all points to something organized—and hidden."

He opened the notebook, revealing a list of names. "Tobias asked about these men. They all gained wealth and influence abruptly. Most were tied to suspicious events."

"How did you find them?" Amelia asked.

"Stubbornness," Ezra said. "Years of digging. The truth doesn't want to be found in this town."

Amelia hesitated. "Could Tobias have uncovered something even you missed?"

"Possibly. He was looking at unaccounted land purchases—transactions with no records, no deeds. If he traced the pattern, it might've made him a target."

A tense silence followed.

Then—a soft sound outside.

A footstep.

Lady Grey growled low in her throat. Clara froze. Ezra moved without speaking, reaching under a stack of books and pulling out a small, worn revolver.

"Stay here," he said.

He crept to the door and flung it open. Outside, the only sign of intrusion was a set of footprints in the soft soil. They led toward the woods before vanishing at the edge of the tree line.

Ezra returned, his expression grim. "You're not the only ones asking questions."

Clara knelt beside the footprint. "Whoever it was, they were careful. Not in a hurry. They were listening."

Ezra holstered the revolver. "Then we need to be careful too. If

Tobias stumbled into Monarch's shadow, he wasn't just chasing a story. He was uncovering a threat."

Amelia looked down at Lady Grey, who sat poised and alert. The town's secrets, long buried, were stirring again—and they had just scratched the surface.

Chapter 5

The Guestbook Clue

Clara Henderson sat at the heavy oak desk in the reception area of the Tumblebrook Inn, the guestbook open before her. A single candle flickered beside her despite the daylight filtering through the windows, casting long, spindly shadows across the ledger's worn pages. The morning had passed in a haze of quiet urgency—discussions with Amelia about Ezra's ominous stories and the hidden roots of the Monarch Society still echoed in Clara's mind. But now, she was hunting something she could pin down. Something real. Something left behind.

The steady ticking of the grandfather clock in the hallway was the only sound. Lady Grey sat motionless on the counter nearby, her amber eyes watchful and unsettlingly alert. Even the inn, usually filled with the warm sounds of clinking teacups and gentle laughter, seemed to have fallen into a hushed suspension—as if the building itself was holding its breath.

Clara leaned over the open guestbook, adjusting her glasses and narrowing her focus. Each name inscribed in the log was like a puzzle piece, a clue waiting to be understood. She was good at puzzles. But this time, something felt different. A pattern was emerging. Subtle at first—names without departure dates, addresses that sounded vaguely familiar.

Her finger ran down the margins. Tobias Greer's name sat near the top of the latest page, recorded with looping precision. But further back, buried in older pages with fading ink, Clara began to notice something odd: several names that had checked in but never formally checked out. She flipped back through a few more years, heart picking up speed.

One by one, she began circling the entries: guests who had stayed no longer than three or four days. Guests who had vanished from the record. No forwarding address. No farewells. One name jolted her memory—Martin Eaves. An article about him had run in the regional news a couple years prior. A missing academic. Vanished while on sabbatical.

Her breath caught. Tobias wasn't an anomaly. He was part of a chain. And each link pointed back to something—something buried beneath Tumblebrook's cheerful façade.

"Amelia," she called softly.

From the dining room, Amelia appeared in the doorway, drying her hands with a tea towel. "What is it?"

Clara turned the book toward her. "This isn't just about Tobias. Look. There are at least five others who never signed out. All of them —historians, real estate analysts, researchers."

Amelia leaned in, squinting at the circled names. "How have we never noticed this?"

Clara tapped the page. "Because there was no reason to notice— until now. But look at the pattern. They all stayed for a few days, then nothing. No sightings. No pickups. Just... gone."

Amelia folded her arms, unsettled. "Do you think they were all here about the Monarch Society?"

Clara nodded slowly. "That's what I'm beginning to believe. Tobias might've been retracing their steps without realizing it. Or maybe he did realize it, and that's what scared him."

Amelia shivered. "We need more. Something concrete. We need

to see Mr. Lark."

Clara closed the book with a soft snap. "Let's go."

Gossamer Fables was nestled like a secret at the corner of Main and Wren, its windows fogged slightly from the contrast of the warm interior and the cool morning breeze. Inside, the air was rich with the scent of parchment, oiled wood, and cardamom from a recently steeped pot of tea. Sunlight slanted in through the windows, catching the motes of dust dancing between tall wooden shelves.

To Clara, this place was sanctuary. She had been working part-time under Mr. Lark since college, and in many ways, the bookshop had become a place of intellectual refuge. Mr. Lark had encouraged her curiosity, pushing her toward mysteries, both fictional and real. He was more than her boss—he was a guardian of knowledge.

Behind the front desk, Mr. Lark looked up from where he was carefully repairing the cracked spine of a dictionary. His silver hair stood on end as always, and his glasses, perched crookedly on his nose, seemed to glint with mischief and intellect in equal measure.

"Well, well," he said, setting the book down. "The wind brings in storm-seekers today."

Amelia managed a smile. "We're hoping you can help us again, Mr. Lark."

He arched a brow. "Curiosity is a dangerous thing in Tumblebrook."

Clara stepped closer, voice even. "We're looking for information about historical land ownership—and anything that might tie into the Monarch Society."

Mr. Lark's jovial demeanor dimmed a fraction. He studied Clara for a long moment, then nodded. "You're sure you want to open that door?"

"We already have," Amelia said. "We can't close it now."

He sighed, then beckoned them to follow. They moved past the public sections of the shop and into the back—into the archive. Clara's pulse quickened. She'd only been back here a few times.

The space was tighter, the air colder, the shelves higher and closer together. It smelled of history and secrets.

Mr. Lark pulled a few volumes, stacking them gently on a side table. "These are land records and a few town-ledger compilations. If Monarch was ever involved in major transfers, the patterns might be in here."

Clara scanned the bindings. One caught her eye—its spine embossed with a fading golden butterfly.

She reached for it. "This one—what's this?"

Mr. Lark's shoulders stiffened slightly. "That's... a delicate piece. It's called The Silent Order. A collection of observations, encoded interviews, fragments. People used to call it the 'Book of Whispers.' But be warned—it doesn't always give answers. Just more questions."

Clara's fingers brushed the cover. The book felt oddly cold, as if it had been resting in a crypt.

"Was Tobias interested in this?" she asked.

Mr. Lark hesitated. "He was. He asked about it just before he disappeared."

The room fell still.

Clara exchanged a look with Amelia, then carefully pulled the book free. "We'll be careful."

Lady Grey, who had quietly followed them in, pawed at the corner of the room. Beneath a loose floorboard, something scraped.

Clara knelt beside the cat. "What have you found, girl?"

With Mr. Lark's help, they lifted the panel. Inside lay a folded page—tucked between old receipts. The ink had bled slightly, but Clara could still make out the elegant script:

"Curiosity lit the lantern. Truth brings the flame. Beware the ones who guard the dark."

A chill settled in her bones.

Amelia whispered, "We're not just reading history anymore."

Mr. Lark slowly nodded. "No, you're walking into it."

Chapter 6

Mr. Lark's Revelations

The quiet air inside Gossamer Fables held a weight of knowledge, an almost reverent hush that deepened the farther Amelia and Clara ventured into the bookshop's back room. Dust swirled in the afternoon sunlight filtering through thick, old-fashioned curtains, casting a golden haze over the piles of books stacked on tables and shelves. The scent of aged parchment, ink, and something faintly herbal wrapped around Amelia like a whisper from another time.

Mr. Lark stood near a long wooden table cluttered with artifacts of history—faded letters, cracked leather journals, and rolled-up maps that bore the brittle edges of true antiquity. His expression was thoughtful as he sifted through the collection, adjusting his glasses with a hesitance that spoke of knowledge long locked away. His slow, deliberate movements added to the tension already thick in the room.

"I suppose," Mr. Lark finally said, "if you've come this far, you deserve to know the truth about the Monarch Society."

Amelia exchanged a glance with Clara, her heart thudding faster. Since Tobias Greer's disappearance, whispers of the secretive group had taken on a life of their own. Now, standing on the cusp of truth, the weight of that mystery suddenly felt very real.

Mr. Lark placed a hand on a heavy tome. The binding was cracked, the cover embossed with a faded golden emblem—the same monarch butterfly Clara had noticed earlier. He tapped the cover with reverence. "The Monarch Society was never just a group of influential families, though that was the face they presented to the town. In truth, they were something far more covert—an organization bound not just by power, but by preservation."

Amelia frowned. "Preservation of what?"

Mr. Lark sighed and pulled over a wooden chair, settling into it with the slow grace of age. "Of knowledge. Secrets. Legacies not meant for public eyes. They safeguarded documents, maps, and artifacts dating back to Tumblebrook's earliest days—before the town even bore its name."

Clara leaned forward, resting her elbows on the table. "And Tobias was after one of these secrets?"

Mr. Lark nodded. He picked up a smaller, plainer book from the table and flipped through its delicate pages until he found the one he wanted.

"Tobias asked specifically about this." He pointed to an illustration—a hand-drawn map, yellowed with age. "It details several landmarks tied to the Monarch Society. Most are forgotten or deliberately hidden."

Amelia leaned closer. The ink had faded, but the layout was unmistakable: Tumblebrook, as it once was. Familiar roads curved into unfamiliar trails. The lake—now serene—was marked with symbols denoting entrances, thresholds, and unknown destinations. Several red markings stood out.

"These markings," Clara whispered. "They're deliberate. This map was updated. Someone else was using it."

Mr. Lark closed the book gently. "That's what drew Tobias here. He believed he'd found a trail that connected Monarch's holdings to a modern pattern of silence—disappearances, falsified records, forgotten lands."

Clara straightened. "This goes deeper than we thought."

Mr. Lark nodded. "Far deeper. Tobias wasn't the first. Over the years, others came. Scholars, journalists, archivists—they asked the same questions, followed similar trails."

Amelia frowned. "Where are they now?"

"Gone," Mr. Lark said. "Some left in the dead of night. Some left belongings behind. Others were never seen again."

He pulled another ledger from beneath the table and flipped through brittle pages. "Martin Eaves, Leonard Finn, Rachel Holloway. All stayed at the inn. All followed this map. All vanished."

Clara's breath caught. "Martin Eaves is in our guestbook."

Amelia's voice was barely a whisper. "So this is more than a theory. It's a pattern."

Mr. Lark nodded grimly. "A dangerous one."

Silence settled. The map. The disappearances. Tobias may have uncovered something real—and paid the price.

"May I?" Clara asked, motioning to the map.

Mr. Lark passed her the book. "Be cautious. Secrets like these don't like to stay uncovered."

Amelia traced a path from the lake to a circle etched at the edge of the forest. It looked unremarkable, but something about it tugged at her memory.

"We need to go to these places," she said.

Clara nodded. "We start with the closest site. Maybe Tobias left something behind."

Mr. Lark's voice lowered. "Take this." He retrieved a folded document—an index of Society symbols. "It may help you decipher what you find."

Amelia accepted it reverently. "Thank you, Mr. Lark. For trusting us."

"I'm trusting your hearts," he said. "Tobias wasn't just a writer. He was a seeker of truth. So are you."

Clara tucked the book under her arm. The time for questions was over.

The time for answers had begun.

Chapter 7

Secret Hideaways

The overgrown path into Tumblebrook Park shimmered with morning mist, the scent of damp earth mingling with pine and moss. Clara and Amelia moved cautiously, the ancient map they'd retrieved from Mr. Lark's archive clutched tightly in Clara's gloved hands. Though the ink had faded in places, the markings were unmistakable. This was where their search began.

Lady Grey padded silently beside them, her silver coat sleek against the underbrush. She sniffed the air, her fur bristling with each alert twitch of her ears. The forest seemed to hush around them—no wind, no birdsong, only the soft crunch of leaves beneath their boots.

"It's too quiet," Clara murmured, scanning the trees beyond the trail.

"I don't like this," Amelia replied, glancing behind them. "Feels like we're being watched."

Clara nodded, turning back to the map. The first location marked in red wasn't far. Labeled *Sentry's Alcove*, it was a place Mr. Lark had once described—a forgotten lookout post from Tumblebrook's earliest days, used when the town was little more than an outpost. If the Monarch Society had chosen it, they had done so for a reason.

As they approached, the woods thickened. Sunlight filtered through the canopy in narrow shafts, and the air grew heavier, saturated with the weight of history. The alcove itself appeared suddenly—a shallow rock shelter nestled between a grove of ancient pines, veiled by vines and low branches.

Clara stopped short. "There," she whispered.

Amelia crouched near a half-erased boot print, the soil still soft from the night's rain. "Someone's been here. Recently."

Clara brushed aside a cluster of leaves and uncovered a faint ring of stones. "And they built a fire," she said, her voice tightening. "This isn't old. It rained last night. The coals haven't scattered yet."

She reached for a nearby stone and turned it over. Etched into the flat surface were precise, angular markings—not decorative, but deliberate.

"These aren't natural," Clara muttered. "This is a cipher. They were communicating—leaving messages."

Amelia leaned in. "About what?"

Lady Grey meowed low and pawed at a moss-covered rock near the fire pit. Clara followed the cat's lead, uncovering another stone—this one marked with a variation of the same symbols.

"They weren't just hiding out here," Clara said. "They were exchanging coded information. Someone else has been using this place."

Amelia exhaled slowly. "Maybe not gold or treasure—but something more dangerous. Evidence."

They fanned out, scouring the alcove's edges and crevices. Clara spotted something wedged between two stones—a scrap of parchment, edges blackened, center fragile but intact.

She pried it loose, reading aloud:

"...the Monarch legacy must remain hidden. If found, it will unravel everything..."

Her voice faltered. "Someone tried to destroy this."

Amelia crouched beside her. "And someone else saved it."

As Clara turned the parchment, her fingers brushed something firmer beneath the underbrush—a charred, leather-bound book. Its cover was scorched, but a faint golden butterfly still gleamed through the soot.

"The Monarch Society," Clara breathed. "This proves it."

She opened the brittle cover. The first pages were ruined, but farther in, the writing endured:

"...safeguard knowledge... trust none beyond the Order... the ruins hold what we have left behind."

Clara glanced at Amelia. "Tumblebrook doesn't have any ruins."

"Not officially," Amelia said. "Maybe that's the point."

Clara nodded. "A hidden place disguised as something ordinary."

Amelia rose, brushing pine needles from her jeans. "If someone tried to burn this, they weren't just hiding the truth. They were burying it."

Clara slid the book into her satchel. "Then we'll dig it back up."

Suddenly, Lady Grey hissed, ears flattened, body rigid.

The forest fell completely silent. No birds. No wind.

Amelia's voice dropped to a whisper. "We should go. Now."

They didn't speak as they backed away from the alcove, their pace quickening. Even after reaching the trail, the sense of unease clung like fog. Clara cast one last glance over her shoulder.

No movement.

But she felt it.

They weren't alone.

Chapter 8

The Forest Intrigue

The woods surrounding Tumblebrook Park stretched endlessly, the towering trees closing in like silent sentinels as Amelia and Clara ventured deeper into the forest. The wind whispered through the branches, rustling the leaves with a hush that made every cautious step feel amplified. The discovery at the alcove still weighed on Amelia—the scorched book, the cryptic warning about the Monarch legacy, and the gnawing sense that they weren't the only ones searching.

Lady Grey trotted ahead, her silver-gray coat blending into the misty morning air. She moved with unmistakable purpose, tail flicking, whiskers twitching. Amelia had long since learned to trust the cat's instincts. Now was no exception. There was a tension in Lady Grey's posture—a silent alert—that made Amelia's skin prickle.

"I can't shake the feeling we're walking into something we're not ready for," Amelia murmured.

Clara, her eyes scanning the weathered map in her hands, nodded. "We've already found more than we bargained for. If the Monarch Society was as powerful as it seems, whoever's protecting their secrets won't take kindly to us poking around."

The trees thickened around them. Sunlight barely filtered through the dense canopy, and the air grew heavy with the scent of damp earth and pine. Every footfall felt muffled, like the woods were absorbing sound. Listening.

Then, Lady Grey stopped.

Her ears flattened. A low growl rumbled from her throat.

Amelia and Clara exchanged a glance, slowing instinctively. Just ahead, partially hidden by thickets and shadow, a small clearing opened before them.

At its center: an abandoned campsite.

Amelia's breath caught. The fire pit still smoldered, faint wisps of smoke curling upward. Around it were signs of a hasty exit—fresh footprints, a crumpled blanket, a half-empty water bottle, scraps of paper dancing in the breeze. The perimeter was marked with peculiar objects: twigs bound in string, small stacks of stones like makeshift totems.

"Someone was just here," Clara said, kneeling by the fire. She touched the ash. "Still warm."

A chill traced Amelia's spine. "They left fast. Too fast."

Her gaze swept the clearing. Everything had the feel of panic—abandoned in haste, as though whoever had camped here fled the moment they sensed they weren't alone. Something caught the light beneath a layer of damp leaves.

Clara reached for it and brushed away the debris. A notebook. She flipped it open, her eyes scanning quickly.

"It's a journal—notes, dates... and names."

She held it toward Amelia, finger tapping a hastily scrawled line:

Meeting scheduled – G.F. & T.G. – URGENT

"T.G.," Amelia whispered. "Tobias Greer."

Clara's frown deepened. "G.F.... Could that mean Mr. Lark? Gossamer Fables?"

Amelia's pulse quickened. "If Tobias was meeting someone from the bookshop, this goes deeper than we thought."

"We need to ask Mr. Lark—directly," Clara said, tucking the notebook under her arm.

Before they could move, a sharp rustle shattered the stillness.

Lady Grey's growl deepened, her fur bristling. Amelia spun toward the sound—just in time to glimpse a shadow slipping into the underbrush.

"Someone's watching us," Clara whispered.

Amelia gripped her arm. "We need to go. Now."

But something glinted in the dirt near the fire pit. Amelia crouched, reaching for it.

A locket. Old. Dented. Its chain broken.

She opened it.

Inside: the initials **T.G.**

"Tobias," she whispered. "He was here."

Clara glanced nervously at the trees. "And he may have met someone who helped him—or betrayed him."

"There's more," Clara said, flipping back through the notebook. "Here: *'the ruins hold what remains.'* That same phrase again."

Amelia pocketed the locket. "Whatever these ruins are, they're important. We need to find them before someone else does."

Lady Grey hissed suddenly, her gaze locked on the woods.

Another flicker of motion.

Amelia's voice dropped to a whisper. "We have to move."

Clara nodded, and together they turned back toward the trail, boots crunching over leaves and twigs. Lady Grey led the way, pausing often to ensure they kept up.

As the trees began to thin and the light returned, Amelia looked back one last time.

The clearing was empty.

But something unseen lingered in the silence.

Tobias Greer had been there. He had discovered something. And someone was desperate to keep it hidden—even if that meant chasing them through the forest.

Whatever the ruins held, they would need courage, clarity, and each other to face what came next.

And, of course, Lady Grey.

Chapter 9

Night at the Inn

The Tumblebrook Inn exhaled a sigh of old wood and stormy stillness as the last hues of twilight deepened into violet. Clara stood at the top of the staircase, the cool banister grounding her as wind pressed against the windows in rhythmic, breathy gusts. Outside, a fine mist veiled the streets, and the distant wail of wind weaving through the trees made the inn feel more isolated than ever.

Despite the flickering fire in the parlor, unease tugged at her— primal, uncanny. Like a page had turned in a book before she was ready.

Lady Grey paced near the hearth, tail twitching, paws silent against the worn floorboards. In the kitchen, Amelia lit a hurricane lantern, her movements deliberate and steady. Each flicker of light cast long shadows across the walls, giving the space a theatrical glow —cozy, but edged with tension. Like a stage moments before the curtain rose.

The power had gone out an hour ago—first a flicker, then a full collapse into silence. At first, Clara had blamed the storm. But now, with each candle's glow stretching shadows farther, the outage felt orchestrated. Not random. As if someone wanted them in the dark.

"This place is giving me the creeps tonight," Amelia murmured as she carried the lantern into the dining room and set it down. The amber light softened her face but couldn't hide the worry in her eyes.

Clara nodded, tugging her cardigan tighter. "Let's go through Tobias's things again. We might have missed something."

They'd collected his belongings after the police completed their initial—and, Clara suspected, superficial—search. Tobias had packed lightly but deliberately: a small suitcase, a worn leather satchel, a neat stack of guidebooks, and a folder of papers. Ordinary at a glance. But nothing about this was ordinary anymore.

Clara spread the contents across the table as the storm muttered outside the windows. The only sounds inside were the hiss of wind and the soft tread of Lady Grey's paws as she leapt onto a nearby bench.

Clara started with the satchel. Inside, a travel-sized notebook embossed with T.G. sat nestled against folded maps and loose papers. Its leather cover was pliable from use.

She flipped through it slowly. The first entries were innocuous—notes about café hours, sunrise over the lake, praise for Doris Finch's blackberry scones. But midway through, the tone shifted.

Pages filled with sketches—symbols, maps, butterfly emblems. Cross-referenced names. Hidden meanings embedded in the everyday.

"These symbols match some of the stones we found," Clara murmured, tracing one with her fingertip.

Amelia leaned over. "They're identical. And here—look." She pointed to a chart. "He was tracking people in town. These initials—*E. Kestrel, M. Underhill, D. Finch... and G.F.*"

Clara's breath caught. "G.F.—from the urgent meeting in the campsite journal. He'd identified them."

"If he met with them," Amelia said quietly, "that could've been the trigger."

Clara turned to the suitcase next. Beneath folded shirts and a toiletry bag was a cloth-bound book. Heavy. Personal. She opened it carefully.

Not a published book—a journal.

"Tobias was documenting everything," she said, skimming the first few pages. "Every conversation, every odd look."

"Read something," Amelia urged, drawing her chair closer.

Clara obliged: "'*June 3rd. D. Finch unusually cagey when Monarch Society comes up. Shifted topic to rhubarb pie. Coincidence? Or rehearsed deflection?*'"

Their eyes met across the table. Each new entry darkened in tone —mentions of being followed, strange cars, missing pages from town archives. Tobias's handwriting, once neat, turned hurried and jagged.

Then came a line that made Clara freeze.

"'*June 5th. Saw same figure by lake again. Tall. Coat collar up. Pretended not to see me. Lady Grey growled before I even heard the twig snap. She knows.*'"

Lady Grey, as if on cue, flicked her tail and moved to sit beside the journal, as though confirming her role in the unfolding mystery.

Clara turned another page. Tucked inside was a receipt from the hardware store: spade, rope, waterproof lantern.

"Not exactly sightseeing gear," she muttered.

Amelia's voice was low. "He wasn't just investigating. He was preparing. Maybe even to bury something."

Clara flipped to a rough sketch—an underground chamber, its entrance partially eroded. Below it, Tobias had scrawled: "Coordi-nates unclear. Possibly near second alcove? Shoreline erosion may have revealed entrance."

Amelia's pulse quickened. "He thought something was out there."

Before Clara could turn the page, Lady Grey's ears flattened. She leapt from the table and bolted toward the parlor.

A sound followed—a floorboard creaked upstairs.

Both women froze.

Amelia stood slowly, lantern in hand. "Probably just the wind," she offered, but her voice trembled.

Clara crept to the foot of the stairs, peering up into darkness. "We should check the windows. Make sure they're locked."

Before Amelia could respond, Lady Grey hurled herself at the parlor window, growling low.

Clara spun toward her. "What is it?"

BANG!

The window slammed shut, rattling the glass. Both women jumped.

Amelia gasped. "Did you see that?"

Clara ran to the pane, heart pounding. Outside, a figure retreated down the garden path. Tall. Coat flapping. Face obscured by the night.

"They're watching us," she whispered. "They've been watching all along."

Chapter 10

Shadows Among Us

The morning dawned gray and heavy, clouds draped low over Tumblebrook like a woolen blanket pulled tight against the earth. Amelia stood by the inn's bay window, a steaming mug of chamomile tea cradled in her hands, watching fog curl over the lake. Her thoughts swirled with it—thick, unsettled. The events of the previous night refused to quiet: the slamming window, the figure in the storm, Tobias's cryptic journal entries. There was no more room for denial.

Someone had been watching them.

Behind her, the inn was too quiet. Not peacefully so—watchfully so. Clara had gone to Gossamer Fables to consult Mr. Lark and dig through old records. Lady Grey dozed on the windowsill, tail flicking now and then, as if sensing the undercurrent of tension that clung to the walls like static. The power was still out. The roads, flooded and impassable, only added to Amelia's sense of confinement.

She set the mug on the mantel and rubbed her arms, though the fire burned steadily. The silence felt unnatural. Not the calm of a small town morning, but something charged. Alert. As though the very walls were listening.

A knock startled her.

She stiffened. The knock was soft—measured, hesitant. She crossed the foyer and peered through the warped, rain-slick glass.

Ezra.

She opened the door. "Ezra?"

"I got your message," he said, voice low and worn. "Figured things must be strange if you're calling on me."

"They've gotten stranger than strange," Amelia said, stepping aside.

He entered with a damp rustle, shedding water from his threadbare coat. His beard was damp, and his spectacles fogged as he looked around the inn with instinctive caution.

"You're sure you weren't followed?"

"No," she admitted. "But we don't feel safe. Something's off."

He nodded grimly and moved toward the fire. "I brought something you should see."

From his satchel, he pulled a weathered leather portfolio and laid it on the table. Inside were sketches, letters, and brittle documents—faded, cracked, and old. "I've gathered these over years. Odd bits of Tumblebrook's history that never made the official records. I thought it was just lore—until Tobias came, asking the right questions."

He spread several pages across the table. Amelia sat beside him, scanning the contents. One image stopped her: robed figures gathered beneath a stone arch, each holding a torch. Symbols lined the arch—like those Clara had photographed in the woods.

"What is this?" Amelia asked.

"An undocumented ceremony," Ezra said. "Most believe the Monarch Society was just an old-money club. But there are whispers of rituals. Covenants. Pacts made before Tumblebrook even had a charter."

He flipped to another sheet—a letter dated 1837, written in looping script:

"*...we must uphold the covenant, lest the land reject us. The seal must remain intact, and the names preserved in silence...*"

Amelia felt the chill run up her spine. "What covenant?"

Ezra's voice dropped. "No one knows for sure. Some say it was for prosperity. Others think it protected them from something darker. But the Society kept their secrets close. Anyone who dug too deep vanished. Or left town, without a trace."

"Just like Tobias," Amelia whispered.

Ezra nodded. "He was obsessed with the seal. The ruins. The symbols. He traced Monarch landmarks through old maps, but something rattled him. He started recording everything obsessively."

For the next hour, they cross-referenced Ezra's findings with Tobias's journal and Clara's notes. A clearer picture emerged—less of a quaint town with a mysterious past, more a place whose foundation was built on secrets and control.

One parchment caught Amelia's eye. A faded oath written in Old English. At the bottom: a name.

Aldric Farnsworth.

Amelia's breath caught. "That's my great-great-grandfather."

Ezra looked sharply at her. "One of the founders. That might explain why you were drawn into this. Bloodlines mattered to them. Still do."

The mystery had turned personal. Her family—her name—was woven into the Monarch Society's legacy.

"There's something else," Ezra said quietly. "Rumors of a vault—hidden beneath the town. Documents, relics, instructions. But the last person to mention it publicly? Gone."

Amelia swallowed. "You think Tobias found it?"

"I think he got close."

When Ezra finally left, Amelia brought Tobias's suitcase into the parlor. Her thoughts raced. What did her ancestors have to do with all of this? Why was Tobias involved—and had he dragged her and Clara into something ancient and dangerous?

She unlatched the case and examined it carefully. If Tobias suspected danger, he would've hidden his most valuable discoveries.

Her fingers found something—a seam slightly raised. A hidden compartment.

Inside: an envelope wrapped in waxed paper.

She opened it.

A black silk patch rested inside. Gold thread embroidered a monarch butterfly within a laurel wreath. Crimson Latin text ringed the edge:

Custodiamus Veritatem — We Guard the Truth.

Beneath it, tucked in the envelope, was a key. Heavy. Ornate. Cold.

The bow bore the same butterfly emblem.

Not just a key.

A message.

Before she could think further, footsteps creaked just outside the door.

Amelia froze.

They didn't knock.

They didn't enter.

After several tense seconds, the steps retreated.

Lady Grey stood in the hall, ears up, eyes fixed on the door.

Amelia exhaled shakily, heart pounding. Then she looked again at the key in her palm.

They were close now. Close to something buried. Something dangerous.

And maybe—finally—the truth.

Chapter 11

A Shared Conspiracy

Clara adjusted her scarf against the wind slicing through Tumblebrook's narrow main street. The fog had clung to the town since dawn—thick, metallic-scented, and heavy—blanketing everything in a shroud of silence. As she passed the grocer's, she noticed curtains twitching, conversations halting mid-sentence. Subtle, but unmistakable.

People were talking.

More importantly, they were worried.

Her first stop was the post office. Old Mr. Thistle greeted her with his usual stiff nod, but his gaze darted toward the door, uneasy. His fingers trembled as he sorted the mail.

When Clara casually asked about Tobias Greer's last mail pickup, he stiffened.

"I'd let that man rest, if I were you," he muttered, voice gravelly. "Some things in this town are better left buried."

Buried.

The word echoed in Clara's mind like the toll of a distant bell. She thanked him and left, resisting the urge to look back.

She made her way to the café. The streets were quieter than

usual, the typical weekday buzz reduced to a murmur. When she stepped inside, the bell chimed, and the scent of cinnamon and fresh bread enveloped her.

It should have been comforting.

Instead, it felt rehearsed.

Doris Finch stood behind the counter, drying a tray, her eyes lifting to meet Clara's. At the window, Harriet from the sewing shop and Martin, the retired park ranger, sat whispering, watching.

"Morning, Clara," Doris said, her cheer bright but hollow.

"Hi, Doris. Just a tea to go."

Doris nodded and turned to the kettle. Clara lowered her voice.

"Did Tobias ever mention the Monarch Society to you?"

The kettle hissed. For a moment, the café went silent.

"Maybe once," Doris said carefully. "Didn't think much of it. Always scribbling in that notebook, asking questions."

"Did he say what he was looking for?"

Doris's smile faded. "Ghosts. And ghosts in this town don't like being disturbed."

Clara didn't press. Doris's tone carried finality. She paid, thanked her, and left.

Even Doris—lover of gossip and rumors—was wary.

That confirmed it more than anything.

Back at her cottage, Clara spread her findings across the kitchen table. Tobias's journal. Her photographs. Notes. Candles flickered, casting long, restless shadows across the cluttered surface. Her laptop, running on battery, displayed her digital annotations of the town map.

As she drew lines between sites Tobias had marked—Monarch meeting places, homes, carved stones—a pattern emerged.

Stars.

Orion's Belt. Down to the spacing.

Her breath caught.

She grabbed an old astronomy book and flipped pages. Other

town sites aligned with constellations: Cassiopeia, Cygnus, Ursa Major.

The town's layout wasn't random. It had been built as a map of the heavens.

Why?

She opened Tobias's journal again. One entry discussed "astral resonance"—the belief that celestial patterns could influence power. He'd theorized that certain rituals or secrets were hidden in towns modeled on the stars.

Clara's heart pounded. What if Tumblebrook was a vault? Not just of history—but of belief. Purpose.

She scrolled further in her notes and cross-referenced lunar cycles. Solstices. Some of the Monarch sites aligned with astronomical events. She traced them on the map again—and this time, another shape appeared:

A spiral.

A ceremonial path? A key?

She whispered, "Were they trying to awaken something—or seal it away?"

Lady Grey jumped onto the windowsill, back arched, tail twitching.

Clara followed her gaze. Beyond the porch, the fog pressed thick against the glass. She saw nothing—but felt everything.

She turned back to the journal. One folded page marked by Tobias bore a list:

Motives: Power. Legacy. Control. Fear. Watch the quiet ones. They guard the loudest truths.

She read it again. And again.

A name stood out—underlined several times. A former councilman who had resigned abruptly and left town. Tobias had written:

"Tried to speak. Silenced."

Clara scribbled it in her own notebook. One more thread.

Another entry caught her breath: "Night at the Inn."

Tobias had written of whispers in the walls. Of Lady Grey staring into corners for hours. He called the inn a vault:

"Not of gold. Of knowledge. A nexus. The seal is not ornamental —it's a lock."

Clara shivered.

Then—

A soft rustle.

She turned.

A slip of paper lay just inside the door. Thin. Clean. Deliberate.

She hadn't opened the door.

Trembling, she picked it up.

Scrawled in red ink:

Dig deeper, and you'll find more than expected.

The message was more than ominous.

It was personal.

She turned it over.

A butterfly. Faintly drawn in graphite.

The Monarch's symbol.

Clara backed away from the door, heart racing. Lady Grey growled, low and steady. The candle flames flickered violently.

She wasn't alone.

Not anymore.

Chapter 12

Voices Beneath the Lake

The wind off Tumblebrook Lake cut sharper than usual that afternoon. Amelia adjusted the collar of her wool coat as gusts sliced through the air, stirring the slate-gray water into restless ripples. Clara stood a few steps behind her, binoculars in hand, eyes fixed on a stretch of shoreline where the land curved inward to form a quiet alcove.

Lady Grey moved like a sentinel along the narrow path, her sleek form gliding low to the ground. Her ears flicked occasionally, attuned to something neither woman could hear—a rhythm laced into the silence.

They had come chasing whispers: fragments pulled from old journals, wary townsfolk's remarks, oral histories passed down like bedtime stories laced with dread. The final clue had come from Mr. Lark that morning, shared over strong tea and lowered voices.

"I thought it was theater," he'd said. "Bonfires, lanterns, strange songs masked as harvest chants. Children laughing. Adults clapping to a beat just slightly... off. But the map in Tobias's journal matched those sites exactly."

Now, Amelia and Clara stood at the lake's edge, where bristling reeds defied the wind and moss clung stubbornly to stone. The air was thick with the scent of damp earth and algae—familiar, but strangely foreboding. A hush blanketed the lake. No birds. No engines. Just the murmur of water and the breath of wind.

Amelia crouched near the shore, brushing away mud and leaves until her fingers met the edge of a weathered plank. Clara helped lift it, revealing a flat stone platform beneath, its surface worn and etched with faint, time-softened symbols. Monarch symbols.

"It's real," Clara murmured.

Amelia nodded. "They've been holding ceremonies here. Maybe for centuries."

Deeper into the cove, they found remnants of fire pits—half-burned logs, rusted iron skewers, scattered green glass shards. A ring of stones formed a near-perfect circle. In its center lay a toppled pillar, carved with runes, half-buried in earth and moss. Around it were offerings: twigs bound in twine, tiny clay figurines marked with butterfly wings and crescent moons.

Lady Grey meowed from the water's edge—urgent, insistent.

Clara turned toward the cat's line of sight. Just beneath the lake's surface, a faint shimmer.

Amelia knelt, reached in, and pulled free a thin bronze disk etched with concentric circles. A butterfly emblem dominated the center, its wings patterned with tiny stars.

"A seal?" Clara asked, crouching beside her.

"Or a token," Amelia said. "Part of something bigger. Or a key."

They laid out the finds on a nearby bench: the bronze disk, the shards, a charred cloth fragment faintly scented with oil and herbs. Along its edge, embroidered in fading gold, was a crowned butterfly.

"These weren't props," Clara whispered. "They were tools."

Movement on the opposite shore drew their eyes. Two women walked the far path, heads bowed. One looked up, caught sight of them, and froze. She whispered something to her companion, who turned quickly. Together, they hurried away.

"Recognize them?" Clara asked.

Amelia shook her head. "But they recognized us."

Fog returned as the day waned, cloaking the lake in slow, gauzy waves. Even the birds stayed quiet.

Back at the inn, they spread their findings on the table. The butterfly symbol appeared again and again. Clara compared it to stonework markings from the courthouse, the library, the inn itself—each one echoing Tobias's journal sketches.

"They left a trail," Clara said. "As if they wanted it found—but only by someone who knew how to see it."

Amelia nodded. "And those who stumbled onto it by accident... disappeared."

That evening, under string lights in the village square, the town looked deceptively festive. Children's laughter mingled with the scent of cinnamon and woodsmoke. But Amelia knew better. Tumblebrook wore its charm like a mask.

They paused outside the old courthouse, its stone façade darkening in the early dusk. Intricate vine engravings climbed its corners. Beneath one window, Clara found a spiral carved into the stone—nearly invisible, unless you knew it was there.

"You believe the rumors?" Clara asked. "About a Monarch promise carved into the foundation?"

"I don't know," Amelia said. "But if it exists, someone still believes in it. Enough to silence Tobias."

Snow began to fall—quiet, gentle flakes that blanketed the street in hush. They turned to leave, crossing the lake path once more.

Laughter echoed nearby. A family emerged from the shadows—parents and two children, cheeks pink from the cold, arms full of bakery boxes. The father nodded. The mother offered a wary smile.

The youngest, a girl no older than six, skipped ahead. She looked up at Amelia, eyes wide.

"My mom says not to talk to strangers," she said with a grin. "But I saw the vanishing man."

Clara knelt. "The vanishing man?"

The girl nodded. "He came out of the water, then—poof! Gone. Like magic. He had shiny shoes and a book. But he didn't see me."

Amelia's heart raced. "When did you see him?"

The girl's mother rushed forward, placing a hand on her shoulder. "She has an active imagination," she said briskly. "Come along."

But the girl looked back, voice a whisper. "He had a butterfly on his coat."

Amelia and Clara stood frozen in the falling snow, breath curling white in the stillness.

Tobias had been here. And he had left more than whispers behind.

Chapter 13

Plans of the Past

The morning after their eerie encounter at the lake, Clara woke with the child's words echoing through her thoughts: "He had a butterfly on his coat." She turned the phrase over again and again as she brewed a pot of strong black tea and settled at her kitchen table, surrounded by Tobias's journal, her own notes, and a growing stack of reference books from Gossamer Fables.

Outside, frost webbed across the glass. The town lay in a cold hush—less serene than stifled. Clara bundled herself in a thick cardigan, the silence pressing in with a weight that felt personal. If Tobias Greer had uncovered something buried, the child's comment suggested he might still be leaving clues behind.

She hadn't told Mr. Lark everything. Though curious and helpful, he skirted discussions when certain family names arose—names carved into the town square's plaques and painted into the portraits in the library's halls. There were still rules in Tumblebrook. Silent ones. Ones that hadn't faded, even after generations.

Clara flipped through her notebook, filled now with star alignments, cryptic symbols, and half-legible scribbles Tobias had left behind. She spread maps, newspaper clippings, and handwritten notes across the table like a paper mosaic. Something was taking shape. A tapestry woven of secrets and symbols. Everything pointed back to the Monarch Society's hidden legacy.

It was time to put names to the shadows.

Her first stop was the town museum beside the courthouse. The curator, Gerald Meyers—a wiry man with expressive eyebrows—recognized her instantly.

"Clara Henderson," he said with a smile. "Haven't seen you since the Midsummer Archive Tour."

"I was hoping to look again at the historical family exhibits," she said. "Specifically ones related to the Monarch Society."

His smile faltered. "That section's a bit... scattered."

"I understand," Clara said softly. "Even heirlooms or tapestries might help."

After a moment, he nodded and gestured her along. They moved past dusty displays and faded placards until they reached a narrow room behind a velvet rope. In one corner, a cloth-shrouded object waited. Gerald pulled back the covering.

The tapestry was exquisite, though dulled with age. Woven in deep greens and golds, it showed a ring of robed figures beneath a great tree. Above them, unmistakable: the crowned butterfly. The figures wore clothing from different eras. One bore the Eastwood crest. Another's robe hem bore the Farnsworth family tree.

Clara stared. "They weren't just chosen. They were inherited."

"Some called it their form of royalty," Gerald said quietly. "Legacy masked as tradition."

In the background, a familiar constellation glimmered—Orion. She scribbled notes. It was confirmation: the society's reach spanned generations, and its descendants still walked among them.

Gerald handed her a small stack of uncatalogued inventory cards. "Some families didn't want their names officially listed."

The names linked families to positions of influence—church boards, council seats, school leadership. Clara's pen didn't stop moving.

Next, she made her way to the eldercare home on Maple Hollow Road. She'd heard whispers about two residents who might know more: Sylvia Bright and Henry Calter. Both had appeared in Tobias's research and in Ezra's stories.

Sylvia welcomed her with a nod. Her room smelled of lavender and old paper.

"You're the book girl," she said. "The one who asks questions."

"I'm trying to understand the Monarch Society."

Sylvia's smile faded. Her fingers twitched against her shawl.

"You don't uncover secrets," she said, "without becoming part of them."

Still, she handed Clara a small brass key from her knitting basket. "Box in the library basement. My father said someone would come for it."

Clara left with her pulse racing. The key felt heavier than metal —weighted with meaning. It was permission. A summons.

Back at Gossamer Fables, the sun spilled through the bay windows as Mr. Lark shelved books near the rear. He looked up as Clara entered.

"Find what you needed?" he asked.

"More than I expected," she replied.

On the counter sat a brown-paper package tied with string. No name. No return address. No markings.

Clara opened it slowly.

Inside: a sheet of thick parchment covered in symbols and hand-written instructions:

"Follow the roots beneath Orion's gaze. The key you hold is not just to a box, but to a path forgotten. Midnight reveals what daylight denies."

Beneath the message, drawn in careful ink, was the crowned butterfly—now paired with a labyrinth.

Her fingers trembled. The labyrinth wasn't decorative. It was a map.

Symbols repeated along its corridors—the same she'd seen etched in stone in the woods and sketched in Tobias's notes. The design wasn't just a place. It was a sequence. A ritual. A path.

She reread the line: *"The key you hold is not just to a box..."*

What if the library basement didn't house an archive?

What if it hid a chamber? A gateway? Something older than the archives themselves?

Her gaze swept the quiet bookshop, suddenly aware of how unchanged it all looked—dust motes swirling in golden light, the hush of pages waiting to be read.

But Clara knew the truth.

Something old was stirring beneath Tumblebrook.

And the time for quiet observation was over.

Chapter 14

Confirmation at the Café

The Tumblebrook Café always smelled like cinnamon, butter, and just a hint of burnt coffee. Amelia Farnsworth stepped inside and took a deep breath of its familiar warmth. For years, this had been her refuge—a welcoming nook where the clink of spoons and the whisper of steam created a constant lullaby. A place where neighbors shared more gossip than grievances, and the sharp chill of the world outside melted into the sweet hum of small-town charm.

But today, as she pushed open the door and ushered Clara in behind her, that comfort felt dimmed. The air seemed thicker, like it carried secrets suspended in the shafts of morning light. Warmer, yes —but also tight. As if the walls were listening.

Lady Grey, against café protocol, padded softly at Amelia's heels. No one had the heart to stop her. The British Shorthair had become something of a fixture around town since Tobias Greer's disappearance. Some whispered she knew more than she let on. Others swore she could sniff out lies. Either way, she found a sunny patch by the window and made herself at home, her tail swishing in slow, deliberate arcs.

Amelia scanned the room. Doris Finch stood behind the counter, her red apron dusted with flour, her expression unreadable. A few regulars occupied their usual seats: Martin Dell hunched over a crossword at the back table; Joyce Hanover knitted by the window; and two retired council members, Geraldine Crum and Lou Pinter, nursed their tea beneath a newspaper that was a day old. Conversation hummed like a distant tide—comforting, but laced with tension.

Seasonal garlands adorned the walls, and chalkboard menus promised spiced cider and fresh apple tarts, but even the cheerful touches couldn't banish the undercurrent of unease. Clara touched Amelia's elbow.

"Still sure about this?"

Amelia nodded. "We can't keep tiptoeing. People know things. We need to ask the right questions."

They ordered tea and warm scones, then settled into a booth in the corner—strategically placed near the regulars. For several minutes, they chatted about mundane things, letting the atmosphere relax. Lady Grey hopped onto the bench beside Clara and curled herself into a regal loaf, her amber eyes watchful.

Then Amelia raised her voice just enough.

"It's strange, isn't it? How Tobias Greer vanished into thin air. You'd think a man like that would leave some kind of trail."

Joyce looked up, her needles pausing mid-row.

Martin grunted. "Writers are slippery. Always chasing ghosts."

Doris glanced over from the counter but said nothing. The café's rhythm stuttered, conversation faltering.

Clara leaned forward. "We think he may have been looking into the Monarch Society."

The shift was immediate. Teacups paused midair. A chair scraped across the floor. Even the old ceiling fan seemed to slow.

"I thought we were done with that old myth," Geraldine muttered. "Bunch of bedtime stories and amateur theatrics."

"Is that what it is?" Clara asked calmly. "Because from what we've found, it was more than that. Meetings. Rituals. Inheritance. People are still honoring those traditions."

Doris moved from behind the counter and began wiping an already-clean table. Her mouth pressed into a thin line. Silence pressed in around them.

"He met someone," she said.

The room froze.

"Tobias," Doris continued. "He came in that morning. Ordered black coffee. No sugar. I asked if he wanted the usual cinnamon bun. He declined. Said he was meeting someone."

Amelia leaned in. "Who?"

"He didn't give a name. But I remember the man. Wore a green scarf. Carried himself like he didn't want to be noticed."

"Was he from around here?"

"Maybe. Maybe not. But he left with Tobias through the back. I always keep one eye on the side door."

The alley. Leading to the old Town Council building.

Clara was already scribbling.

"Could he have been on the council?"

Doris's gaze flicked briefly to Lou and Geraldine.

Amelia caught it. "You know who he was."

Doris dropped her rag and folded her arms. "Look, this town has its way. Tobias asked questions no one wanted to answer. Sometimes, questions cause more harm than silence."

Joyce's knitting resumed, faster now. Martin folded his paper with crisp finality.

Lou cleared his throat. "You girls don't know what you're poking."

"Then tell us," Amelia said. "Help us understand."

Lou stared at his tea. Finally, he spoke. "There were meetings. Not just the Monarch stuff. Recent ones. We tried to keep it symbolic. But not everyone agreed."

"Who wanted more than symbolism?" Clara pressed.

"I can't say. But Tobias asked. Two days later, he was gone."

Another silence fell—thicker, deeper.

Then a voice from the front table, soft and shaken.

"There were meetings under the library," Joyce said. "With robes. Candles. They said it was theater, but it didn't feel like a show. Not when they asked for blood oaths."

Even Lady Grey looked up sharply.

"You attended one?" Clara asked gently.

Joyce gave a small nod. "Years ago. My father brought me. Said it was legacy. But there were rules. Things we weren't supposed to speak of."

Doris sighed. "There's always been a line between pageantry and power. Somewhere along the way, some folks forgot which side they stood on."

Amelia scanned the room. These people weren't just wary—they were afraid. Bound by silence, unsure whom to trust.

Geraldine's hands trembled as she lifted her mug. "He asked the wrong questions. And someone decided it was easier to make him disappear than answer them."

The bell above the door jingled.

A stranger stepped in, nodded, and took a seat at the counter. He ordered black coffee in a voice that carried without effort. He didn't glance around, but his presence shifted the room.

The conversation was over.

But a wall had cracked. And through that crack, light had begun to shine.

Chapter 15

Unmasking the Intentions

The morning sunlight filtered through the tall windows of Gossamer Fables, painting golden rectangles across the worn floorboards like celestial clues left by a benevolent universe. Clara stood behind the front counter, methodically sorting a new delivery of rare books. The scent of aged paper mixed with the warm, nutty aroma of brewed coffee wafting in from the back, creating a peaceful ambiance she usually relished. Today, though, peace eluded her. There was an unspoken urgency vibrating beneath her skin, a tension that threaded through her bones.

Her fingers trembled slightly as she peeled back the flaps of a cardboard box. Her mind was not on titles or catalog numbers. It was miles away—buried beneath the library, echoing in whispered oaths, lingering in the eyes of townspeople who had said too much or not enough. Her body might have been in the bookstore, but her spirit wandered dark corridors and flickering candlelit chambers of the past.

The café meeting two days prior had cracked something open. Clara hadn't slept much since. Every phrase, every sideways glance, every name uttered in hushed tones replayed in her mind like a haunting lullaby.

"There were meetings under the library. Real ones. With robes. Candles."

Those words weren't the ramblings of a paranoid old woman. Clara was increasingly convinced they were the breadcrumbs that led to the heart of Tumblebrook's most guarded secrets. She felt as though Tobias Greer had left behind invisible threads, and she was finally beginning to tug the right ones. Today, one would unravel a tapestry of hidden intentions.

She set the box on the counter and began removing the volumes. Most were unremarkable—weathered travel memoirs, a collection of coastal recipes, a 1930s guide to herbal tinctures. But as she lifted a dusty folio of poetry, she felt a subtle shift in the box's bottom panel. Something wobbled beneath it. Clara paused, heart stuttering, then reached in and tugged gently.

A false bottom lifted free with a hesitant creak.

Nestled beneath was a thin leather-bound book, nearly black with age. It was tied shut with brittle twine, the pages yellowed and curled at the corners. No title. No markings on the cover. Clara swallowed hard. Even before she opened it, she felt its significance humming in her hands.

Heart pounding, she carried it into the back office. Lady Grey, her quiet companion, trotted dutifully behind her and hopped up onto a side chair with the dignity of a feline archivist. She meowed softly, a low, throaty sound that Clara had come to associate with serious discovery.

Clara placed the ledger on the desk and carefully untied the twine. The pages crackled like dried leaves as she turned them.

At first, the contents seemed indecipherable. Lines of symbols, odd slashes and loops, numbers in strange sequences. But some pages had annotations in faded ink—single words in cursive, scattered dates, cryptic initials.

Clara's breath caught. The symbols weren't just gibberish. They mirrored the shorthand Tobias Greer had used in his own notes to describe Monarch rituals and coded communications. She retrieved Tobias's journal from her satchel and laid it open beside the ledger. The resemblance was uncanny.

She whispered, "This was how they communicated. Directives. Orders. Instructions... hidden in plain sight."

The entries spanned decades. She flipped to a page marked with a butterfly stamp—crisp, deliberate. Beneath it, coded phrases repeated over the years, each tied to a date and a name:

G.F. – Compliant. H.C. – Monitor closely. E.L. – Asset established. Trust level moderate.

Gossamer Fables. Henry Calter. Ezra Lark?

A chill ran down her spine.

She underlined the names and started constructing a key to decipher the symbols. Within an hour, she had matched at least nine individuals from Tobias's research with corresponding entries in the ledger. What emerged was more than just a record of messages. It was a blueprint of control.

She documented a network of influence where Monarch operatives had infiltrated every institution in Tumblebrook: the school board, the historical society, local charities, even the festival committees. Clara found references to decisions made behind closed doors—controversial zoning changes, strategic land acquisitions, public works delays, even abrupt closures of family-run businesses. These weren't coincidences. Each one had a date. Each date matched a directive in the ledger.

They hadn't just preserved tradition. They had steered it, manipulated it, ensured that only those aligned with their vision rose through the town's ranks. The ledger made it clear that nothing was arbitrary. Every motion passed at a council meeting, every grant denied, every election result—it was all part of a greater scheme.

What disturbed Clara most was the manipulation of the town's narrative. Public events that were presented as spontaneous community efforts were, in reality, orchestrated acts with specific intent.

Even the annual Founder's Day Festival had been used to disseminate coded messages through speeches, performances, and even the patterns of the parade route.

She discovered notations indicating who had attended each year's events and who had not—marked as *"enthusiastic," "indifferent,"* or *"needs persuasion."* There were stars next to certain names, and circles around others. This wasn't mere ritual. It was strategy. It was surveillance.

Her pen raced. The magnitude of what the Monarch Society had done—and was still doing—was overwhelming. Tobias had only scratched the surface. Clara was excavating the bones beneath the garden. She could feel her pulse in her fingertips, a silent drumbeat of both dread and determination.

The book included references to operations titled *"Bluebell"* and *"Echo Root"*—terms Tobias had circled in his own notes. "Bluebell," it seemed, had to do with the repurposing of public lands; *"Echo Root"* with the tracking of lineage and influence. She found entries marked with red ink from the 1970s that linked Monarch involvement in school curriculum adjustments and the quiet removal of dissenting educators.

In that moment, she realized something profound—this wasn't just about Tobias. This was about Tumblebrook itself. The Monarch Society had rewritten its very history.

She leaned back, stunned. "This... this changes everything."

Just then, a soft knock came from the front. "Clara?" Amelia's voice echoed gently. "You need to see this."

Clara gathered the ledger and walked out, Lady Grey gliding along silently. Amelia stood near the display table showcasing handcrafted local art. She was kneeling beside a wooden sculpture Clara had always found too odd to be endearing—an ivy-wrapped crescent moon mounted on a block of unfinished pine. It had sat there for years. No one remembered who had donated it.

"She won't stop staring at it," Amelia said, glancing at Lady Grey, who was perched just inches away, her eyes locked on the sculpture with unwavering intensity.

Clara crouched beside her. She examined the base of the sculpture and noticed, tucked beneath a curved ridge, a tiny notch—barely the size of a fingernail.

She pressed it.

With a soft click, the sculpture tilted slightly backward, and a thin panel of the wall behind it popped open. Dust spilled from the crack. The scent of cedar and old paper followed.

Behind the panel was a hollow space.

A compartment.

A secret chamber.

Amelia gasped. "How long has this been here?"

Clara reached in slowly and pulled out a velvet pouch, faded and stiff with age. Inside, she found a set of ornate keys and a folded parchment sealed with wax—the same crowned butterfly emblem.

With trembling fingers, she broke the seal and unfolded the parchment. It wasn't a letter—it was a map. A hidden layout of the building, revealing a crawlspace beneath the floorboards and a door that connected to the foundation wall of the adjacent property—one Clara didn't recognize. The annotations were written in the same hand as the ledger's.

Along the edge of the map was a phrase written in Latin: *"Veritas sub umbra manet"*—The truth remains beneath the shadow.

She exchanged a glance with Amelia. "We need to see what this opens."

Amelia nodded. Lady Grey flicked her tail once and stared pointedly at the map, as if to say: You've come this far. Don't stop now.

Chapter 16

Sculpted Secrets

Amelia Farnsworth stood beside the narrow opening in the wall behind the sculpture, heart pounding like a mallet against antique wood. Dust spiraled through the slant of sunlight across the floor, catching in her lashes as she squinted into the dark. Clara crouched beside her, the velvet pouch and wax-sealed parchment still clutched in her hands. Lady Grey sat poised nearby, tail flicking, eyes unblinking—like she'd always known this place was here.

"Are you ready for this?" Clara asked.

Amelia took a breath. "We've come too far not to be."

The passage was barely wider than a closet—tight, musty, and walled with uneven stone. Just beyond it was a small chamber, its walls rough and cool to the touch. A rusted lantern hung askew from a bent nail, coated in cobwebs. Clara flicked on her flashlight, the beam slicing the gloom.

Shelves carved into the stone revealed rows of rolled blueprints, brittle ledgers, and plastic sleeves warped with age. A canvas map stretched across the far wall, pinned in place with rusted nails. Its edges curled like dry parchment, but the faded outline of Tumble-brook was unmistakable.

Amelia stepped closer and opened one of the ledgers. A puff of dust lifted. Inside were entries written in looping ink: architectural details, land records, and notes dated back to the 1800s.

"These aren't just records," she murmured. "They're instructions."

Clara leaned in. "And not just for buildings. They mapped the entire town—with intent."

Amelia pointed to a note in the margin: *Monarch approval required.*

Another read: *Discreet chamber—model after root cellar.*

"They didn't just influence Tumblebrook," Clara said. "They designed it—with secrets in mind."

Lady Grey trilled, brushing against Amelia's calf like a silent agreement.

They knelt and unrolled the larger maps. Dozens of locations were marked with symbols they recognized from Tobias's notes: tunnels, hidden rooms, passageways connecting the library, court-house, inn, and even rural estates.

"This is an entire version of Tumblebrook we've never seen," Amelia said softly. "A town beneath the town."

Clara pulled a folded parchment free. Tobias's handwriting covered the page—meeting summaries, family names, and a disturbing theory.

"He believed the Society's 'sacrifices' weren't metaphors," she whispered. "Evictions. Business closures. People cast out—for balance."

Amelia's throat tightened. "Chosen losses... to protect tradition."

She reached for another document—a stamped decree bearing the Monarch butterfly and the motto: *In Unitate Lux*—In Unity, Light. The message underneath described deliberate manipulation of the town's development for a so-called greater good.

Clara unfolded another envelope addressed to a former councilman. Red slashes ran through the names of dissenters. Many were familiar—former shopkeepers, school staff, residents who had vanished from memory.

Lady Grey pawed delicately at a nearly hidden scroll behind the shelf. Clara retrieved it carefully, and gasped.

Blueprints. Extensive ones. Faded ink traced a web of underground corridors. They reached beneath nearly every major building in town.

"These are escape routes. Ceremony chambers. Storage vaults," Amelia said. "All part of the infrastructure."

"They weren't accidents," Clara added. "This was engineered."

For the next hour, they cataloged documents, photographing delicate pages and setting aside key artifacts. Each new page peeled back another layer of the town's constructed identity.

"This isn't folklore," Clara said, her voice quiet but sure. "This is systemic."

Amelia nodded. "Tobias was right. And he disappeared because of it."

Lady Grey darted to a dark seam in the wall—one they hadn't noticed before—and tapped her paw against the edge. Amelia followed, running her hand along the stone until she found a latch.

Another hidden recess.

Inside was a stack of journals, a cluster of sealed envelopes, and a single ornate key. The journals were nearly a century old, filled with a strange blend of mundane notes and cryptic references to underground gatherings and "silent correction."

Clara opened one and inhaled sharply. "Landmarks no longer listed on maps—the quarry, the lighthouse. Tobias mentioned these. Everyone said he was imagining things."

"They weren't imagination," Amelia said. "They were part of the network."

She couldn't bring herself to say *sacrifice*. But she saw it in Clara's eyes too.

They laid out everything on the stone floor—maps, entries, artifacts. The story was clear now: Tumblebrook wasn't just built with stone and timber—it was shaped by secrecy, molded by ideology, upheld by ritual. The tunnels weren't just physical—they were psychological. A legacy of control passed from hand to hand in silence.

From her perch, Lady Grey gave a short, sharp chirp, glancing once more at the narrow entrance they had come through.

The message was unmistakable.

The truth was no longer hidden.

But the real journey had only just begun.

Chapter 17

Unearthed Passageways

Clara descended the cellar stairs beneath Gossamer Fables, each footstep echoing off the stone like a whispered warning. Her flashlight cast a thin blade of light through the musty dark, catching on dust-veiled crates, rusted cabinets, and bowed brickwork that looked ready to collapse. The air hung thick with mildew and something older—forgotten.

Behind her, Amelia followed with the blueprints rolled beneath one arm, her breathing shallow, her boots scuffing the worn stone. Even Lady Grey padded softly ahead, ears tilted forward, her movements sharp with purpose.

Tumblebrook had fallen strangely quiet. The air was too still. The lake, which usually danced with ripples, sat motionless—glassy and unbothered. Clara felt it in her chest: a tension, as if the ground itself waited for what came next.

Lady Grey stopped at a southern wall obscured by shelving and a moldering box labeled *"Lantern Festival Programs, 1973."* She sniffed, pawed. Clara followed, heart quickening. There—just visible in the beam—was a hatch: iron-framed, sealed tight, rimmed in grime. Faintly, beneath the dust, a butterfly had been carved into the metal.

Clara knelt. The latch stuck, then groaned open with a grinding protest. Cold, metallic air rushed out, damp and ancient. Below, narrow stone steps fell into darkness.

"Ready?" she asked.

"Only one way to go," Amelia said.

They descended, flashlights flickering across veined stone and rotting timbers. Along the walls, carvings emerged—symbols Clara recognized from the coded ledger. They passed relics: rusted tools, cracked shoes, crates stamped with names from the town's founding families. Moisture beaded on the stone. Silence pressed in.

One sign, half-swallowed by decay, read: *Echo Root Access – Authorized Only.*

"Echo Root," Clara whispered. "From the files. An operation."

Amelia marked it on the map.

Deeper still, the tunnel widened into a high-ceilinged chamber ribbed with wooden supports and crowned with murals: robed figures in solemn procession, flames burning in ritual circles. The paint had faded, but the meaning remained.

At the center stood a locked iron cabinet marked with the Monarch butterfly. Amelia pulled the ornate key from her coat. The lock resisted, then clicked open.

Inside: ledgers, folders, sealed boxes.

Clara opened a folder sealed in red wax—council minutes, ceremonial schedules, reports dating to 1903. Another contained incident logs: business closures, sudden relocations, obscure zoning laws. Families erased. Homes reassigned.

Amelia read from a parchment: "*Ceremonial Sites Reaffirmed: Library Sub-Basement, Founder's Fountain, Church Cellar. Offerings to align with generational cycle.*"

"Offerings," Clara murmured. "Not metaphorical."

In a lower drawer, a scroll revealed precise geometric tunnels beneath the town. Nodes were marked with Monarch butterflies, others with fire, keys, stars.

Lady Grey froze.

A sound. A step.

They snapped off the lights.

Stillness.

A shadow moved at the chamber's edge. Clara's heart raced. Amelia's grip found her wrist.

"We're not alone."

Silence stretched. The presence lingered, then retreated.

They packed what they could: the ledger, blueprints, a few folders. As they turned to leave, Clara spotted a fresh note pinned behind the cabinet. Crisp, black ink on thick paper.

This is your final warning. Truth has a cost.

Below it: a sigil. A broken crown wrapped in a serpent.

Amelia paled. "That's not Monarch. That's something else."

Clara folded the note. "They want us to stop. Which means we're close."

They climbed out into the cellar, blinking in the dim daylight. Lady Grey paused at the threshold, gazing back.

Clara closed the hatch behind them.

Neither spoke.

But in their silence was something louder than fear: determination. The truth was no longer buried. And now, someone was listening.

Chapter 18

Revelry at the Ritual

The scent of mulled cider and roasted chestnuts clung to the crisp October air as Amelia Farnsworth stepped into the bustling square of Tumblebrook. Autumn had adorned the trees in resplendent hues of amber and crimson, their leaves swirling like confetti in the breeze that danced between vendor booths and lantern posts. From a distance, the annual Harvest Festival appeared as idyllic as ever. But tonight, Amelia saw it differently.

Children darted past with sticky fingers and painted cheeks, their laughter mingling with the soft strains of fiddle music drifting from the gazebo. Elderly couples sipped cider and admired the hand-carved gourds and scarecrow displays, while teenagers juggled apples near the cider stand. It should have felt like home. But to Amelia, the warmth and charm of the scene only heightened the sense of unease that tugged at her.

She clutched her satchel tightly, its contents far weightier than any scarf or sweet she might have purchased: a camera, Tobias Greer's deciphered notes, redacted Monarch files, and a battered notebook filled with symbols. All of it pointed to this night—and to something buried beneath the celebration.

Clara stood at her side, bundled in a dark peacoat, her scarf tucked close against the chill. Her eyes, half-shielded beneath the brim of her knit cap, scanned the crowd. "You're certain the symbols align?"

"The festival. The full moon. The lanterns in the northern quarter," Amelia murmured. "It's all here. Tobias called it the Evening Offering. He believed it happened during the festival, hidden in plain sight."

Lady Grey, nestled in a side pouch with a mesh window, emitted a low trill. Even she seemed restless, ears swiveling as if attuned to vibrations no one else could hear.

They moved deliberately, blending in. Clara purchased cider, Amelia examined bookmarks. They greeted familiar faces with smiles and nods, all while keeping a mental tally of the known Monarch names scattered among the crowd. Shopkeepers. A school board chair. One of the assistant pastors from St. Agnes.

At the edge of the square, the lights faded. Beyond the lanterns, a path curved toward the old orchard and the mill ruins—both marked on Tobias's map with a crimson crescent. It was there they would find what the town tried to forget.

The laughter behind them dimmed as they followed the leaf-strewn trail, flashlights kept pocketed. Moonlight guided their steps. The further they walked, the colder it grew—not just in temperature, but in sensation. The silence was heavy, reverent, almost as if the trees themselves held their breath.

And then: torches. Flickering flames embedded in the ground like sentries. Hooded figures gathered in a wide circle before a mossy stone platform. Masks concealed their faces—butterflies, owls, wolves—each hand-painted with uncanny detail. The flames cast long shadows that danced and swayed with the murmured chants.

Amelia and Clara crouched behind a toppled column, breath tight. Amelia's hand found the lens of her camera and began snapping photos in silence.

The figure at the center—taller than the others, mask crowned with gold filigree—raised a staff marked with the Monarch butterfly. The chanting ceased.

"Tonight," the voice intoned, altered through some device, "we honor the Keepers before us. We offer silence, memory, and service. From stone to stream, from breath to bone."

Clara scribbled the words quickly, her fingers trembling.

A second figure stepped forward, carrying a velvet bundle. Within it, a ledger—much older than the one they'd found. The leader began reading from its pages: names, dates, oaths. Then, a smaller cloaked figure was led into the center. The initiate. The circle closed in, hands linked, a medallion pressed to the youth's chest.

Amelia's heart pounded. A ritual. An indoctrination.

Clara whispered, "They're choosing new members. Tobias was right."

Suddenly, a sharp crack echoed through the woods. A snapped branch. Or something more.

The leader paused. Masks turned. Tension rippled.

A cry rang out, followed by chaos. Torches fell. Robes fluttered. The circle shattered. One mask slipped, revealing the face of a councilman Amelia had seen last week buying scones at Doris's café.

Amelia grabbed Clara's hand. They ducked low as a satchel dropped near the altar, its contents spilling: maps, old keys, a ledger fragment. Clara snatched it quickly and stuffed it into her coat. Lady Grey hissed from her pouch, then went silent.

They ran.

Branches clawed at their coats as they fled, heartbeats thudding in their ears. Behind them, the sounds of scrambling footsteps and shouted warnings chased them through the dark.

They didn't stop until the lantern glow of the festival reappeared between the trees.

No one looked their way. The music continued. The scent of cider returned.

But Amelia knew: nothing would ever taste as sweet again.

Chapter 19

Bonds of the Fearful

The town of Tumblebrook looked the same as ever the next morning, bathed in a deceptive hush beneath the rising mist. Clara Henderson, walking beside Amelia through the main square, felt the weight of everything they had seen pressing down on her shoulders. The secrets beneath the surface felt closer than ever—whispering warnings beneath every flag flutter, every smiling shopkeeper's greeting, every rustle of leaves. The town wasn't just hiding something. It was trying not to see.

Clara's thoughts kept returning to the ceremony—the masked figures, the chants, the ledger. It haunted her like a dream she couldn't shake, each image sharp with meaning. There had been familiar faces, masked but not fully hidden, and symbols that matched everything she and Amelia had uncovered. The ritual hadn't been folklore. It had been continuity. She tightened her grip on her notebook. The Monarchs weren't relics. They were architects.

They had barely slept. After the chaos at the mill, they had spent hours poring over the contents of the dropped satchel in the inn's attic room—curtains drawn, lights low. The materials were damning: maps showing tunnel expansions from the 1970s, cryptic letters between unnamed Monarch members, and frequent references to "keepings" and "bindings." A brass key etched with odd symbols. A wax seal bearing the butterfly insignia. Clara had cataloged everything meticulously, her mind buzzing with patterns and connections, while Amelia brewed pot after pot of tea and Lady Grey curled atop the older maps, twitching as if dreaming of secrets too deep to voice.

Amelia watched the cat, wondering what Lady Grey sensed. It couldn't be coincidence—the cat always appeared at the turning point. Amelia had once believed herself simply an innkeeper. Now, her name—her family—had surfaced again and again in the Monarch records. How deep did her roots go? And what would it mean if she was part of what she was trying to dismantle?

They had discussed whether to go public. Or at least to confide in someone outside their circle. But every path carried danger. The Monarchs weren't just history. They were power—active, insidious, disguised in plain sight. What Clara and Amelia had uncovered didn't just revise the past. It unraveled the present.

Even in daylight, as the square shimmered with celebratory banners and laughter, Clara could feel it: a pulse of fear, humming beneath the town's surface like a wire under tension. People knew. Or suspected. The silence wasn't accidental—it was tactical. And it was growing.

At the florist, Elsie, who had once shared whispered observations about town council patterns, wouldn't meet Clara's gaze. She handed over the bouquet Amelia had ordered with a too-bright smile and disappeared into the backroom. The door clicked locked before it even shut.

The same at the bakery. The same at the schoolhouse. Pleasant faces, pleasant words—but the life behind them had dimmed. Even the children were quieter, their games subdued, their laughter cautious.

"They know," Clara murmured as they stepped out of the post office, the door chime sharp as glass.

"Or they're protecting someone," Amelia added. "Or both."

Lady Grey trotted beside them, unusually close, tail low, eyes alert. Her usual curiosity had given way to tension.

Conversations stalled as they passed. Neighbors turned away. Even the regulars at the inn had become guarded, their conversations hushed, their departures early. The weight of suspicion followed them like a shadow.

They lingered at the general store. Clara tried to strike up a conversation with Peter, the young clerk who had once mentioned strange deliveries.

"How's your mother, Peter?" she asked gently.

Peter gave a polite but distant smile. "Well enough, Ms. Henderson. Excuse me, I need to restock."

As they stepped outside, Amelia whispered, "Someone turned the town against us. This isn't just fear—it's pressure."

Two council members stood on the library steps, their conversation dying the moment Clara and Amelia approached. Eyes followed them. A neighbor who once brought over cookies now crossed the street to avoid them.

They found Doris Finch in the café's pantry, pretending to organize preserves. Her hand trembled as she picked up a jar.

"Doris," Clara said quietly. "We're not here to cause trouble. But you've always had a nose for what's hidden. And we think—"

"Don't." Doris' voice was low but firm. She stared at the back window. "Stop asking questions out loud. People are listening. Always listening."

"You told us Tobias met with a council member," Amelia said gently. "Do you know who it was?"

Doris hesitated. "I thought I could help. I really did. But now it feels like I'm under a spotlight. I can't risk it."

"Even one detail could help," Clara urged. "People are scared for a reason."

Doris leaned closer, her voice barely a whisper. "The Monarchs never left. They just changed names, changed meeting places. But they're still here. Watching."

Amelia's eyes narrowed. "Watching—or recording?"

Before Clara could respond, Lady Grey—perched on the counter —let out a low, warning meow. Her golden eyes were fixed on a wall shelf.

Clara followed her gaze.

A wooden butterfly hung above a stack of recipe books—festive, decorative. But up close, Clara saw it for what it was: a replica of the Monarch emblem. Subtle etchings beneath the wings. Familiar lines.

She pulled it down. Behind it: a faded symbol. A circle, with a triangle at its center—drawn exactly like Tobias had sketched it. A marker. A warning. A message.

"There's more," Amelia said, brushing at the wall.

More sigils appeared—initials: *M.L., D.S.* A butterfly, drawn upside down. It was a layered code. A record of allegiance. Or betrayal.

"Doris," Clara asked softly, "why was this hidden behind the emblem?"

Doris's mouth tightened. She looked between the two of them for a long moment. Then: "Because there are things I'm afraid to know. And the Monarchs... punish curiosity. They always have."

A beat passed.

Clara's voice was a whisper. "They didn't just disappear, did they?"

Doris shook her head. "No. They were made to disappear."

Lady Grey growled low, leaping from the counter to stand between the women and the pantry door. Her fur bristled.

The message was clear.

The danger wasn't coming.

It was already here.

Chapter 20

Controlling Forces

The clouds rolled low over Tumblebrook that afternoon, their shadows creeping across rooftops and winding between the eaves like hushed secrets. The town had taken on a restless stillness, as though waiting for something—anything—to disturb the illusion of peace. Amelia Farnsworth stood in the reading room of the inn, Lady Grey curled at her feet, her soft purring the only sound in the room. Her fingers hovered above a pile of letters spread across the oak desk, each one yellowed with age and scrawled in the same crisp, deliberate script.

Clara had left a short time earlier to follow up on one of the names they'd discovered behind the butterfly plaque. Amelia had stayed behind, drawn to the unsettling gravity of the correspondence they'd received that morning—an anonymous envelope slid under the inn's back door. No return address. No note. Just a dozen folded pages that felt heavier than paper.

Each letter was addressed to a different member of the Tumblebrook Council—some names she recognized, others less familiar. The contents detailed proposed decisions, land disputes, festival budgets —and, most chilling of all—civic appointments. Every policy appeared pre-approved by an entity referred to only as "The Circle," a term that radiated power cloaked in secrecy.

The same insignia marked the bottom of each page: a stylized butterfly enclosed within a triangle.

Monarch.

Amelia sat heavily in the chair, the cushion sighing beneath her. Lady Grey looked up and meowed softly, as if to ask, "What now?"

Amelia whispered, "We were never meant to find this."

The betrayal settled in like fog. She had believed in Tumblebrook —its warmth, its community, its charm. But these letters cast everything into shadow. This wasn't just corruption. It was orchestration. If Monarch's hand had guided every major decision for generations, how much of the town's identity had been curated? Or worse— engineered?

Lady Grey rose and stretched, her paws pressing into Amelia's lap like an anchor. Amelia scratched behind her ears, grounding herself in the cat's quiet reassurance.

She needed answers. Urgently.

That afternoon, Amelia walked the silent halls of Town Hall. Clara had promised to meet her shortly, but for now, Amelia moved alone through its solemn hush. It was too quiet—too composed. Like a cathedral built for order, not prayer. Her boots echoed along the marble floors past shuttered offices and sepia-toned portraits of mayors long gone.

In the archive room, behind glass cases, Amelia found the town charters. With a borrowed key from a clerk she'd known since childhood, she unlocked one of the oldest volumes and began to read.

The ink was ghostly, the script ornate. But threaded through the formal language, Amelia began to spot echoes of Monarch ideology. "Continuity through stewardship." "Decisions rooted in heritage, maintained by the unseen hand." Once-innocuous phrases now read like coded mandates. Control cloaked in tradition.

At the back of the volume, a list of the town's first council members. Three initials circled in faded graphite: *M.L. D.S. T.C.*

Her breath caught.

The same initials etched behind the butterfly plaque. Clara had been right. This wasn't coincidence. It was a trail. Monarch hadn't just influenced Tumblebrook. It had founded it.

The implications left her dizzy. The town's legacy had been sculpted not by democracy, but by quiet inheritance. Secret oaths. Selective inclusion. Silenced opposition. Local tradition, Amelia now realized, was a performance of power.

The door creaked behind her. Clara entered, windblown and flushed.

"I spoke to Ezra," she said. "He confirmed it. There was a meeting house—long gone—where the council and Monarch met as one. Their decisions were ritual. Their ceremonies policy."

"And now?" Amelia asked.

Clara hesitated. "Now they're fragmented. Some families cling to the traditions. Others deny them. But the influence? It's still here. Hidden in symbolism. Protected by lineage."

Amelia straightened. "Then we dig it out."

For the next hour, they laid everything bare. Letters. Notes. Ciphered entries. Patterns emerged—five-year cycles, bloodline initiations, town events aligned with clandestine gatherings. Even zoning ordinances favored Monarch-connected properties. Surnames repeated across grant recipients, festival chairs, council rosters.

Amelia traced a web linking civic decisions to Monarch affiliations. Clara layered Tobias's notes on top. The alignment was undeniable: the governing framework of Tumblebrook and the architecture of Monarch were mirrors. A century of control disguised as custom.

"This isn't heritage," Clara said quietly. "It's choreography. They aren't preserving the town. They're preserving their grip on it."

Lady Grey paced at the window, pausing only as a car rolled slowly past—an odd presence this late at Town Hall. Clara glanced up but saw only their reflection in the lamplight.

They were still deep in discussion when the door opened once more. A figure stepped through—silver-haired, straight-backed, wrapped in a green coat that smelled of cedar and age.

Mrs. Gwendolyn Harrow.

Retired librarian. Memory like steel wool. Tongue sharper still. A woman who had once claimed to memorize every banned book in the state archive "for balance."

"I heard you've been stirring dust where it ought to lie," she said, her cane tapping once on the wood floor—a punctuation neither kind nor cruel.

Amelia and Clara stood, uncertain whether to apologize or thank her.

Mrs. Harrow opened her bag and withdrew a manila envelope.

"My brother was one of them," she said. "Not that he ever admitted it. Found this in his effects. Thought someone might need to see it, eventually."

Inside the envelope: a photograph. Black and white. A group of young men and women stood before a stone building, each bearing a butterfly pin.

Dated 1972.

At the center—Tobias Greer.

Amelia's breath caught.

"That's impossible," Clara murmured. "He'd be too young. That photo's fifty years old."

Mrs. Harrow nodded. "The man you knew wasn't the first. Tobias is a name they pass down. Sometimes through blood. Sometimes through choice. But always with purpose."

Amelia gripped the photo. "Then what he told us... everything he wrote..."

Clara finished for her. "It wasn't journalism. It was testimony."

Silence settled over the room like snowfall.

At the edge of the room, Lady Grey uncurled from her patch of sunlight. She blinked once, then let out a soft, knowing purr.

They had crossed a line.

There would be no turning back.

Chapter 21

Monarch's Witness

The low hum of fluorescent lighting in the archives cast an eerie lull over the municipal records room. Clara Henderson sat cross-legged on the carpeted floor, surrounded by an ever-growing fortress of brittle manila folders, dust-laced genealogy tomes, crumbling newsprint, and leather-bound ledgers that seemed to hum with old secrets. The air was stale, thick with disuse, as if the room itself held its breath. Dust hovered in golden shafts of light slanting through arched windows, catching the glint of paper clips and the edges of old photographs.

The photo Mrs. Harrow had handed them hours ago—now reverently encased in a clear plastic sleeve—rested beside Clara on a spread-open volume of Tumblebrook town records. Every time she looked at it, that creeping sensation crawled up her spine. The butterfly pins. The formal, unsmiling faces. The stone façade behind them. But most unsettling of all was the man at the center.

Tobias Greer.

Or the one who wore his face.

Clara gently flipped another page, her eyes methodically combing through surnames and annotations scribbled in fading fountain pen. Her notes filled multiple pages now—long, looping arrows linking names, years, events, and symbols. One entry she circled again and again:

Tobias Greer: No birth certificate. No census entry. No voter registration. A ghost.

Yet his presence had been undeniable. He had walked Tumblebrook's streets, eaten at the café, stayed at the inn, interviewed townsfolk, and left behind notebooks brimming with cryptic clues. Now he was gone. Swallowed, perhaps, by the very mystery he had tried to unravel.

Lady Grey stirred beside her, leaping down from a nearby table to land softly atop one of the older ledgers. The British Shorthair blinked slowly, then pawed at the corner of the photograph's sleeve. Clara smiled faintly and gave her a scratch behind the ears. The cat's presence grounded her—a thread of normalcy in a world rapidly unraveling.

Clara turned to the microfiche machine and threaded a new reel. This one contained issues of the Tumblebrook Gazette from 1968. As the screen flickered to life, a bold headline stole her breath:

MISSING YOUTH BELIEVED TO HAVE LEFT TOWN—NO FOUL PLAY SUSPECTED.

The accompanying photograph showed a wiry seventeen-year-old with intelligent eyes and a faint, sardonic smirk. His name: Linus M. Greer. Clara stared at the image, her heartbeat thundering.

Same bone structure. Same eyes. Could it be? Linus Greer—another iteration?

Her mind raced.

Linus M. Greer → 1968 disappearance → returns as Tobias? Or was Linus the original?

She scanned more reels, locating records of property transfers. A land deed signed by a Linus M. Greer appeared in 1973. Then again in 1981, under the name Tobias L. Greer. Every eight years, the pattern repeated. And with each cycle, a name vanished, replaced by another—similar, adjacent. Greer wasn't just a surname. It was a role.

Then a darker realization formed.

What if the disappearances weren't about removing threats—but anointing them? What if the Mercury cycle wasn't just a calendar, but a mechanism for transformation? A ritual of rebirth masked as mystery.

She leaned back, dizzy with the thought. The air felt colder. Her breath fogged the microfiche glass. A creak echoed in the rafters above. The archives felt more like a tomb than a sanctuary now.

A knock sounded at the door. Clara jumped.

The records room creaked open. Amelia stepped in, cheeks pink from wind and rain. She held out a folded sheet of paper.

"This was under the front door."

Clara rose and took it. The parchment was thick, smooth, expensive. The Monarch seal was etched in obsidian-black ink.

She unfolded it slowly.

The Mercury cycle draws to a close. Silence is owed. Witnesses will be judged.

Amelia watched her reaction. "It's a threat."

Clara swallowed hard. "It's more than that. It's an ultimatum. They know we're too close."

They sat together, Clara spreading her findings across the wide table. She explained the Mercury timeline, the Greer iterations, the disappearances. Amelia listened, silent but attentive, her fingers idly tracing one of the butterfly stamps in the margins.

"The Monarchs don't just hide power," Clara said. "They perpetuate it. They recycle it. They preserve it like a relic in flesh. Each cycle... it's as if someone is chosen."

"And Tobias?"

"I don't know if he was trying to stop them or if he was the next vessel. But he knew something. He knew about the cycle. Maybe he was chosen. Or maybe he tried to break free."

Amelia's gaze shifted to the microfiche screen. "Then we finish what he started."

Lady Grey stretched and gave a low, insistent meow. Clara

followed the cat's gaze to the base of a bookshelf behind them. A faint glimmer caught her eye—something metallic wedged between the baseboard and the cabinet.

She reached down and pulled it free.

A key. Old. Brass. With a butterfly insignia carved into its head. The teeth were oddly shaped—jagged, almost ceremonial. Not designed for a house or drawer, but for something forgotten.

They stared at it for a long moment.

"Where does it lead?" Amelia whispered.

Clara looked back at the photograph. At Tobias's unreadable expression. Then down at the key, the symbol shimmering faintly in the dim light.

"Somewhere we're not supposed to go," Clara said. "But exactly where we need to be."

Chapter 22

Unmasking the Past

The morning fog clung to Tumblebrook like a secret unwilling to part with its keeper. It wrapped around the trees, settled over rooftops like a veil, and muffled the usual sounds of morning life. The inn sat quiet, bathed in the soft gray glow of a cloud-covered sky, its windows still beaded with dew. Inside, the warmth of lamplight filled the parlor where Amelia Farnsworth stood barefoot on the braided rug, surrounded by Tobias Greer's remaining belongings, carefully arrayed across the antique coffee table. Journals. Postcards. Napkins with half-finished thoughts. Clippings. Doodles. Annotated blueprints. The man had left behind a breadcrumb trail so deliberate and intricate, it might have been a maze.

She stood unmoving for a long moment, eyes drifting over the contents, as if by mere observation she could absorb Tobias's intentions. This wasn't just sleuthing anymore. It wasn't about idle curiosity or hosting etiquette. It was personal. The thread Tobias had tugged had unraveled not just a mystery but the very tapestry of Tumblebrook itself. What began as an investigation into a missing guest had become an excavation of truth. Her truth. The town's truth. And possibly, its salvation.

Her fingers hesitated over a leather-bound journal, one of the oldest. She opened it gently, reverently. The pages, yellowed and uneven, gave off the scent of ink and old revelations. Her breath caught. In the margin of one page was a symbol she now recognized as Monarch—the butterfly in the triangle, surrounded by concentric circles like ripples in a pond. Beneath it, Tobias had written in tight script: *What they erase, I will rewrite.*

Upstairs, Clara remained asleep, finally collapsed after a night poring over maps, coded transcripts, and matching initials to old rosters. The girl had tenacity, a mind sharp enough to rival Tobias's. But Amelia had always been the early riser, the quiet contemplator. Mornings like this were sacred—a time for coffee, reflection, and the stillness of thought. But today, that stillness rang loud with unease.

She flipped to another journal. Tobias's entries weren't written chronologically, but in recursive swirls—memories surfacing like bubbles in deep water. Dates drifted past sketches and ciphers, each layered with coded meanings. Some pages were written in prose, others as poetry. A recurring phrase appeared across multiple volumes: *Legacy shapes perception.* Sometimes it was circled, other times underlined three times. Once, it was etched into the margin with what appeared to be blood-red ink.

Amelia traced those words with her fingertip.

Turning the page, she found a detailed timeline. Handwritten. Cross-referenced. Terrifyingly thorough. A Monarch-aligned council vote in 1953 that shifted zoning lines to favor one family's estate. A charity drive in 1976 where the funds disappeared into the creation of a *"Civic Reserve Fund"*—later used to purchase forest land that would never be developed. A school curriculum rewrite in 1984 that quietly removed Tumblebrook's indigenous and pre-colonial history, replacing it with romanticized settler tales. Each event manipulated, adjusted, tailored to reinforce a version of the town that suited Monarch's vision.

Below the timeline was a quote Tobias had scrawled: *Control history, and you control the heartbeat of the present.*

Amelia sat back, stunned. She felt the rug beneath her heels, grounding her. It wasn't just about power—it was about identity. The Monarchs hadn't just governed—they'd rewritten the script. They had become the curators of collective memory.

She thought of the inn. Of her grandfather. Of the land it stood on. Had her ancestors knowingly aligned with Monarch ideals? Or had they simply made peace with a system they didn't fully understand—one that had offered prosperity in exchange for silence?

The deeper she read, the more disturbed she became. Tobias's notes were both exhaustive and poetic. He had backed observations with snippets of official documents, quotes from long-forgotten town meetings, and interviews with now-deceased residents. He'd traced odd alterations in property records, inconsistencies in family registries, and the redirection of community funds into projects that benefited only a select few.

Tumblebrook, Tobias's writings suggested, wasn't just a town. It was a stage. The Monarchs were the playwrights, the directors, and the critics.

She turned to a page with a short but haunting paragraph:

I was not meant to unravel this. I was meant to continue it. But I cannot. I see the faces of those who vanished, feel their silence stretching into mine. If I stay silent, I become them. If I speak, I betray a legacy I never asked to inherit.

Her breath hitched. Tobias had not just been an investigator—he had been indoctrinated. Perhaps unwilling. Perhaps once complicit. Perhaps chosen. But something had broken in him. Something human and irrepressible.

She thought of the townspeople—Mrs. Harrow with her guarded eyes, Doris Finch and her barbed gossip, even old Ezra and his cryptic warnings. How many had known? How many had merely suspected but looked the other way? Had they been afraid? Bought off? Or simply convinced that silence was safer?

A creak on the stairs signaled Clara's descent.

"You're up early," Clara said, rubbing sleep from her eyes.

Amelia gestured to the journal without looking up. "Couldn't sleep. There's too much here."

Clara joined her on the rug, scanning the open pages. "Is that the timeline?"

"It's more than that," Amelia said. "It's proof. That our town's history has been edited—revised in real-time by people with an agenda. What we think we know—what we've always been told—it's all a crafted version."

Clara's brow furrowed. "Then it's time the original version came to light."

Together, they spread the journals across the coffee table, layering Tobias's entries beside their own notes and Mr. Lark's annotated history. Dates aligned too perfectly. Names recurred—sometimes masked, sometimes rebranded. Monarch wasn't a club. It was a bloodline. A shadow bureaucracy. A living document of control passed from hand to hand.

Amelia turned to another journal—one marked with a gold ribbon. It was older than the rest. The leather was cracked and stiff. Inside, the handwriting was distinct. Slanted. Finer. Almost fragile. At the front, a name: *Eleanor G. Farnsworth.*

Her great-grandmother.

The air left her lungs.

She flipped through the pages with a trembling hand. Eleanor's journal was personal, laced with guilt and confession. It spoke of candlelit meetings in basements. Of whispered deals and vows of silence. Of a belief that they were preserving the town.

I told myself we were protecting the town. But at what cost? I hear whispers in my sleep—names I cannot forget. Their stories lost because we chose to bury the truth beneath a well-manicured lie.

Amelia pressed her hand to her mouth. Her family had been involved.

Not as bystanders. As architects.

Lady Grey padded into the room, tail high, and leapt gracefully onto the windowsill. Her amber eyes tracked something unseen, her posture sharp with intention. Then she jumped down and walked purposefully toward the writing desk in the corner—a piece Amelia hadn't touched in weeks.

Lady Grey sat beside it, placed a paw on the bottom drawer, and gave a low, insistent meow.

Amelia raised an eyebrow. "You think I've missed something?"

She crossed the room and knelt, pulling open the drawer. It appeared empty—until she reached back and her fingers brushed paper. Thin. Slightly stiff. She drew it out slowly.

An envelope. Addressed in a familiar hand. *To Tobias Greer.*

She exchanged a look with Clara, whose eyes were wide with curiosity.

Carefully, Amelia opened the envelope. Inside was a single sheet of parchment. Cream-colored. Edges trimmed with gold. The handwriting was elegant, looping.

You were never meant to disappear. You were meant to choose. The door remains open. The question is—will you walk through it, or close it behind you forever?

There was no signature. Just the butterfly seal pressed into the bottom corner.

Chapter 23

Divided Allegiances

The clouds over Tumblebrook churned like thoughts in Clara Henderson's mind. She stood at the edge of the lake, her boots biting into the frost-tipped grass, her eyes tracing the curve of the shoreline where whispers of the past still lingered. Lady Grey paced nearby, tail high, like a silver ghost threading through mist. It had been a week since they'd uncovered the timeline in Tobias's journal and the letter meant for him, and nothing about the town felt the same. The wind whispered differently now—like it carried secrets rather than breeze, like it knew something it wasn't yet ready to share.

Clara had always believed in logic, in systems and patterns, in the idea that truth was a puzzle waiting to be assembled with enough diligence. She had built her life around certainty, preferring neat stacks of facts and rows of evidence to the chaos of hearsay and emotion. But Monarch had shattered that neat order. It had shown her that even truth could be reprogrammed—massaged into myth, bent to convenience. Her once-tidy notebooks, filled with neat lines and orderly bullet points, were now bursting with contradictions, redacted names, and questions scribbled into the margins like cries for help. The pieces had grown too complex, too entangled in human hearts, legacies, and unspoken loyalties.

Now, the trail had led them deeper—not just into history, but into the minds of those who had quietly written it. The problem was no longer just about uncovering the truth. It was about choosing who to trust. Who might still be loyal to the lie—and who had already begun to question it.

Inside Gossamer Fables, where the comforting scent of old books clung to the air like worn wool, Clara and Amelia sat across from each other in the hidden reading room—Mr. Lark's private refuge tucked behind the employee shelves. It was silent except for the hiss of the radiator and the rustling of parchment. A corkboard behind them had become a makeshift evidence wall, layered with strings and index cards that connected decades of secrets like the veins of a spider's web. Lady Grey dozed in the corner, twitching occasionally in her sleep, as though even her dreams were steeped in Monarch's mysteries.

"There are fractures," Clara said, her voice quiet but certain. "In Monarch. Splinters. Tobias hinted at them in his entries, and I think some of the older members are disillusioned."

Amelia tilted her head. "You think they'd talk?"

"They might," Clara replied. "Especially if they feel betrayed. Power doesn't stay consolidated without resentment. Monarch's leadership has shifted over time—slowly, but enough to push out those who remembered when it stood for something else."

They had made a list. Not names—yet. Just roles, historical connections, patterns of behavior. People who had once defended the society loudly and now remained suspiciously quiet. One name circled in Clara's journal more than any other: Alden Pike.

Former town clerk. Widowed. Lived alone in the house with the blue shutters. The man had been loyal to Monarch for decades, but he'd retired early and removed himself from town affairs in recent years. Tobias had visited him twice before disappearing. That detail had stuck with Clara like a splinter she couldn't ignore.

That afternoon, Clara approached Alden's modest house, tucked between pine trees on the edge of town. The sky was bruised with the promise of snow. The windows were dark, the chimney cold. She hesitated before knocking, her breath visible in the chilled air.

When he opened the door, Alden looked smaller than she remembered. His shoulders were hunched, his eyes weary—not just with age, but with a burden he had carried too long. Time seemed to have folded around him, aging him in creases of memory and regret.

"Miss Henderson," he said cautiously. "You're Clara, aren't you? From the bookshop."

"I am," she said, stepping into the porch light. "And I think you knew Tobias Greer."

A pause. A flicker of something in his eyes.

"I knew someone by that name. But he had others."

That was all the confirmation she needed.

"I believe he trusted you," she said gently. "And I believe Monarch doesn't want people like you to speak. But we're not here to silence anyone. We're trying to bring the truth to the surface."

Alden hesitated, his eyes flicking toward the woods beyond the driveway. Finally, with a sigh that seemed to come from his bones, he opened the door wider.

"Then come in. But if I speak, you must understand—I once believed in what Monarch stood for. I still believe in some of it."

"Most people did," Clara replied softly. "That's why it worked."

The house was dimly lit, filled with worn furniture and walls lined with framed town certificates, sepia photographs, and old commendations. The air smelled of cedar and old tea. A few antique clocks ticked in various corners, some in sync, others not, echoing like ghostly heartbeats in the silence. Over mismatched mugs, Alden spoke in a low voice, often glancing at the windows as if Monarch's shadows could still reach him there.

"There was a time Monarch meant stewardship," he said. "Guardianship of heritage. We were supposed to protect what was sacred. But somewhere along the line, preservation turned into control. Leaders became gatekeepers. The truth was rationed, reshaped. Secrets became currency."

"Were there others who felt the same?" Clara asked.

Alden nodded. "We weren't many. A few of us called ourselves the 'Quiet Hands.' We didn't oppose Monarch outright, but we kept records. Safeguards. In case... in case the society turned tyrant. Tobias found us. Or maybe he was always one of us."

He reached beneath the cushion of his armchair and pulled out a folder wrapped in wax paper. Clara's heart pounded. Inside were brittle notes, copies of meeting minutes, maps with strange markings. Proof.

"He said the cycle was breaking," Alden added, almost whispering. "That something was going to change. And then he vanished."

They spent the afternoon cataloging Alden's recollections, drawing out names of those who might still be alive, still willing to speak. Clara filled page after page of her journal—sketching connections, underlining places Tobias had visited. She took photos with her phone, organizing files to be cross-referenced later with what they had collected at the inn. Each note, each recollection, each shaky admission became part of something bigger—a chorus of resistance quietly forming beneath the surface of the town.

It was her first taste of a possible unraveling of Monarch—not through confrontation or protest, but through testimony. Through confession. Through the slow, painstaking reassembly of truth from the pieces that had been deliberately scattered.

It felt oddly like justice. And for the first time, Clara didn't just feel like a puzzle-solver. She felt like a voice for the silenced.

That night, in the bookshop's back room, Clara and Amelia reviewed the growing web of names and information. The corkboard had expanded to the side wall now, and red thread looped like a nervous system across pinned photographs and notecards. Amelia watched Clara with admiration and concern, her expression solemn.

"There's no going back after this," she said.

"I don't want to go back," Clara replied. "I want people to know. And I want Tobias's voice to echo louder than their silence."

Just then, the bell above the front door jingled. Clara and Amelia exchanged a look.

A figure stood in the shop, wrapped in a dark wool coat, face obscured by the brim of a hat. In their gloved hand was a small recorder and a bundle of worn journals bound with twine.

"I heard you're collecting stories," the figure said, voice rasped with age but filled with conviction.

Clara stepped forward. "Are you ready to give one?"

The figure nodded.

"I've stayed quiet long enough."

Chapter 24

Disavowed Drawings

The wind off Tumblebrook Lake had a sharper bite that morning, one that hinted spring was not quite ready to arrive. Amelia Farnsworth clutched her coat tighter and tucked her scarf into her neckline as she approached Ezra's cabin, nestled deep within a thicket of leafless birch and towering pines. The path was slick with thawed frost and fresh mud, but she pressed on, guided not only by resolve but by something else—an ache, a need to make sense of the truth unraveling around her.

In her gloved hand was the note—precise script, unsigned, left beneath the inn's back porch door. It contained only a time, a location, and one line: "The drawings never lied."

Amelia hadn't seen Ezra, the artist-hermit, since early winter. Their last encounter had ended in cryptic mutterings and a warning not to ask too many questions about things buried. But now, with Monarch's veneer cracking and Clara buried in ledgers and whispered testimonies, Amelia needed something concrete. She needed the images—the raw, irrefutable record of what had been seen.

She knocked once. Twice. Silence. On the third knock, the door creaked open on its own, groaning like it had secrets of its own.

Inside, the cabin smelled of pine sap, turpentine, and the dust of long-kept truths. Sketchbooks were stacked haphazardly across tables and windowsills. A strange stillness hung in the air—like the place existed out of time.

Ezra hunched at a wide table under a single lamplight, his hands stained with graphite. His voice came without turning.

"You came."

"You called."

He glanced up, eyes sunken but sharp. "They say art is interpretive. But it's more honest than words. Words can be rewritten. But drawings—drawings remember."

He gestured her forward. Her pulse fluttered in her throat as she stepped into the room, into the thrum of decades of hidden witnessing.

Laid out across the table were sketches—shaded with care, each page a silent scream. Men in suits exchanging envelopes. Shadows bending around council chambers. Symbols she recognized from Tobias's journals: the butterfly, the eye, the threefold seal.

"These are Monarch?" Amelia asked, her fingers grazing the edge of one that showed a faceless figure looming over bowed silhouettes.

Ezra nodded. "Some I witnessed. Some I was told to illustrate. Their version. But I never stopped making mine. The unapproved ones."

He handed her a thick folio. On the front, in aggressive graphite: **DISAVOWED**.

Amelia opened it carefully. The scent of old paper and charcoal rose like smoke. Inside: a story told in shadows.

A child peeking from behind a curtain while elders toasted a silent contract.

A field—public once, now fenced and guarded.

Her breath caught as she turned a page: the inn. Sketched with uncanny precision. Only labeled not as "Tumblebrook Inn"—but as Site 6. Below it, a hidden compartment beneath the stairs.

Ezra watched her face. "They used it. Your family made it easier. Whether they knew or not."

Amelia's stomach twisted. Her home—a nest of secrets.

She thought of her grandfather. His late-night murmurs about the town council. Traditions he'd called "necessary." Had he known? Had he helped?

She didn't have time to spiral. A sharp rap sounded at the door. Ezra stiffened.

"Who knows you're here?"

"Only Clara, and she—"

The door opened. A woman entered—middle-aged, understated, the type who existed quietly at every town gathering. Familiar but forgettable.

Her scarf trembled in her hands. "They're panicking. The loyal ones. But others... they want out. They just don't know how."

Ezra's eyes narrowed. "Council?"

"Briefly. Enough to see what they're willing to erase. Tobias came to me. I turned him away. I was afraid."

She stepped forward and laid a small notebook on the table. Names. Locations. Hidden files. Amelia's gaze flicked to the sketches still in her hands. Proof layered upon proof.

Later, back at the inn, dusk bled across the horizon. Lady Grey lay curled on the windowsill, one paw twitching in her sleep.

Amelia opened the drawer beneath the staircase—the one where Tobias's journal had first been found. She reached beneath the false bottom and retrieved a bundle of his unfinished writings.

The first page bore a scrawl, underlined twice:

THIS ENDS WHERE IT BEGAN.

Beneath it: a half-finished paragraph. The ink smudged, frantic.

It warned of a final gathering—one meant to cement a revised history of Tumblebrook. Not just a meeting. A ritual. A closing act in the town's longest play of silence.

And it was set for two days from now.

Chapter 25

Connection of Truths

The morning dawned with an eerie stillness, as if the very air in Tumblebrook was holding its breath, waiting for truths long buried to rise. Clara Henderson moved through the hushed expanse of Gossamer Fables like a scholar on the verge of completing a great thesis. Each creaking floorboard beneath her step, each rustle of parchment, felt weightier than it had the day before. Her fingers trailed across the spines of books, brushing away thin veils of dust that shimmered in golden sunbeams. The shop's warmth belied the sharp truths emerging from its quiet corners, and yet Clara welcomed them.

There was no more guessing now. The puzzle pieces they had so painstakingly gathered—Ezra's stark drawings, Tobias's fragmented journal entries, cryptic communications, whispered confessions, old land deeds, hidden folios, and coded ledgers—had begun to form something formidable. Not a perfect image, but one defined enough to reveal Monarch's silhouette looming over every inch of the town's foundations. The breadth and depth of the conspiracy was astonishing. It wasn't just about a missing man anymore. It was about a legacy written in shadow—an invisible architecture woven into the town's policies, beliefs, and even celebrations.

Clara set up camp at the rear study table, a sprawling surface where chaos began transforming into order. Papers lay in concentric rings: hand-copied transcripts of interviews, annotated town registers, Ezra's sketches of secret meetings, photographs of commemorative plaques and historical artifacts, excerpts from Tobias's final writings, and even rubbings from tombstones she and Amelia had taken during an impromptu late-night walk through the cemetery. The story was coming into focus. It was a tapestry of voices across decades, threads slowly woven into a narrative too dangerous for Monarch to leave untold. With each connection she unearthed, her certainty deepened. The tipping point had arrived.

The silence around her was meditative, broken only by the hum of the old radiator and the occasional groan of the shop settling into its age. Clara worked in a near-trance, moving papers, aligning time-lines, pinning thread from one document to another on the corkboard she had taken over entirely. Her notes had grown into a web of connections—dates, family trees, properties, and patterns that showed something undeniably methodical. Monarch hadn't just been operating in the background—they had been orchestrating from the center all along.

An hour passed before Amelia joined her, balancing a tray with two steaming mugs and a flaky croissant dusted in powdered sugar.

"You've been here since before dawn," Amelia murmured, setting down the tray. Her voice carried the weight of shared weariness and hope. "Did you sleep at all?"

Clara offered a small shake of her head. Her eyes were clear, focused. "We're almost there. We have what we need—what Tobias was chasing. Now we just need to make sense of it in a way no one can deny."

The two women huddled together under the shop's amber lighting, tracing and retracing the tangled threads Monarch had so carefully knotted over generations. Clara's methodical mind picked apart the symbols—each butterfly, crown, and eye repeated in both ceremonial invitations and financial records, echoing across decades. Amelia leaned in, quietly voicing recognition whenever something aligned with her memories of the inn or town events.

"Look at this," Clara said, sliding an old property register forward. "This transfer happened in 1913. Three signatures. And next to each—these." She pointed at symbols hand-drawn in faded ink.

Amelia squinted. "They match Ezra's renderings. Even the placement."

Clara nodded. "It wasn't just ceremonial. These people weren't acting independently. Monarch embedded its control into Tumblebrook's governance from the start. They rewrote ownership, bent inheritance laws, redirected funding. This was a coordinated strategy masked as tradition."

They both sat back, stunned by the sheer scope.

"It's not just a conspiracy," Amelia said softly. "It's a legacy."

Clara's voice was firmer now. "Then we need to break the cycle."

Throughout the day, they compared more documents—highlighting familial connections between town leaders and Monarch signatories, revisiting earlier interviews now laced with context they hadn't recognized before. Testimonies that once seemed vague now pulsed with significance. Even old town festival programs were revisited; Clara found hidden Monarch symbols printed subtly in borders, and names of families who had long since vanished from Tumblebrook.

They consulted Mr. Lark, who quietly passed along a hidden stack of books from the restricted section—accounts penned by townsfolk whose reputations had been quietly tarnished and whose properties had conveniently changed hands. Tobias had found these too. Clara noticed his initials scribbled in the margins. A few of the books even had pages missing—pages they later found tucked between boards under Mr. Lark's counter, hidden away like illicit knowledge.

By evening, they returned to the inn, folders clutched tight. Lady Grey, ever perceptive, followed closely, her ears flicking with the electricity of the moment. Clara laid everything out in the inn's drawing room. A timeline took shape—marked with pins and thread, a visual narrative of manipulation and power. Across the table, eras and events aligned in ways that had never been publicly acknowledged. They saw the same surnames again and again, entwined with major decisions and council decrees.

"There's one final link missing," Clara murmured, her brow furrowed.

Amelia looked up from a set of schematics. "What do you mean?"

"Tobias's notes. They reference a chamber—something he called the final archive. He said it was the root of all deception. A place where the first truths were rewritten. The line that stuck with me: 'beneath the history that buried the truth.'"

Amelia drew in a breath. "The council building."

Clara nodded slowly. "The basement. The foundation hasn't been altered since the 1800s. Tobias believed there was a chamber there, hidden behind a false wall."

Just then, Clara paused. "Wait..." She rifled through a folder and pulled out a crudely sketched blueprint Tobias had drawn. It showed the council building's layout—but one room was marked only with a question mark. Scribbled next to it were the words: 'Silence written in stone.'"

Amelia leaned in. "Could that be the chamber?"

"I think it is," Clara whispered. "I think that's where it all began —where the founders laid the groundwork, literally and figuratively. That chamber holds the original documents. The first real agreements. Maybe even names."

They sat in silence for a moment, the magnitude of the discovery heavy in the air. Lady Grey hopped onto the armchair beside them, letting out a single, low meow—as if in warning or approval.

"If we're right," Amelia said, "then what's in that chamber could destroy everything they've built."

"Then we go tonight," Amelia said finally. "Together."

"And reveal what Tobias died trying to uncover," Clara added.

Clara glanced toward the fireplace, where Lady Grey lay curled like a sentinel, her eyes half-closed but alert. Tobias had nearly uncovered everything. His work had been tireless, obsessive, and heartbreakingly close. Now it was their turn to finish it. And this time, they weren't alone. Clara sensed a current shifting in town—people who had once turned away were beginning to glance back. Monarch's grip was loosening.

As Clara began to pack the folders and arrange their findings into a portable ledger, she paused for a moment, her fingers lingering on Tobias's final page. Written in the corner, barely legible, was one more phrase she hadn't noticed before:

All truths find their keepers.

That night, long after the streets had emptied and the town had quieted into its usual hush, Clara and Amelia stood outside the council chambers. The building loomed before them, its facade bathed in the soft glow of streetlamps. Lady Grey padded ahead of them, tail high, as if she too understood what was about to unfold.

They moved quietly down the side alley, guided by Tobias's sketch and their own resolve. Clara produced the key they had discovered weeks ago—a rusted, ornate thing that had remained a mystery until now. It slid easily into the maintenance entrance lock.

Inside, the air smelled of old stone and varnished wood. They moved swiftly through the empty corridors, heading for the basement. Clara's pulse quickened as they approached the far wall—the one Tobias had marked with the question mark.

Amelia ran her hand along the cold plaster, pausing when her fingers found a hairline seam. "Here," she whispered.

They worked together, pressing and pulling at the edges until a section of the wall shifted inward with a soft groan. A narrow stairway descended into darkness.

Lanterns in hand, they descended.

The chamber at the bottom was small but profound. Stone-lined, windowless, forgotten. In its center, a long table covered in dust bore piles of parchment, ledgers, and an iron-bound chest emblazoned with the Monarch crest.

Clara stepped forward, brushing dust from the top document. Her breath caught.

"It's all here," she murmured. "Original land grants. Meeting records. The names of those who rewrote this town."

Amelia opened the iron chest. Inside lay a single leather-bound journal, unmistakable in its age and significance. Across the front, stamped in gold:

Tumblebrook Founding Ledger.

The air felt charged, brittle. The truth lay in front of them—not fragments, not guesses, but the undeniable record of how power had been brokered and bartered.

Amelia met Clara's gaze. "It's time to rewrite the ending."

Chapter 26

Autonomy Against Authority

A melia Farnsworth stood in the center of the inn's great room, her cold tea forgotten in her hands. Morning sunlight streamed through the lace curtains, casting dust motes in golden shafts that made everything feel more fragile, more exposed. The evidence was everywhere—on the long oak table, across the walls, in the open ledgers, annotated maps, journal excerpts, and countless photographs. Tumblebrook's quiet veneer had cracked, and now the pressure to act pressed hard against Amelia's chest. Her heart beat not with panic but with the clarity of purpose, sharpened by the fire of awakening.

Lady Grey wove around her ankles like a silver specter, sensing the unease in every breath Amelia took. The previous night had drawn them to the precipice of history's deepest vaults, and the chamber they were to visit held the promise—or threat—of truths powerful enough to destroy reputations and reorder the town's understanding of itself. Amelia had always believed in the strength of community, in the slow beauty of preservation. But now she understood: preservation—once her guiding principle—had been weaponized into silence. It no longer protected; it erased. Monarch's version of history had stolen autonomy from generations.

She paced the room slowly, her mind spinning as she passed each corner now transformed into an evidence board. Tobias's handwriting stared back at her from every page, like echoes of a mind that had never stopped chasing the truth. And now that torch had passed to her.

Yet she also knew that tearing down power without a plan was reckless. Before they could act, Amelia knew they had to build a coalition. She wasn't so naïve as to think unveiling Monarch's secrets would be enough. Power had roots in fear, in tradition, and in the comfort of silence. To shake that foundation would require unity, trust, and a network stronger than the one they meant to expose. Exposure without reinforcement would invite chaos, and that was something she couldn't allow. She wanted change—but not collapse.

By midday, she and Clara had drafted a list of individuals they believed could be swayed—those who had murmured doubts in their testimonies, or those whose families had once been erased from Tumblebrook's story. They needed not just witnesses, but participants in a transformation. They went door to door, knocking not just on homes but on hearts, reigniting questions long buried. Their efforts were methodical, but compassionate. With every conversation, they planted seeds of possibility.

They began with Ezra, the reclusive artist whose drawings had catalyzed much of their understanding. He arrived at the inn wrapped in his signature wool coat, the smell of turpentine and pine still clinging to him. Amelia welcomed him with a nod and gestured toward the evidence wall.

"You were right about everything," she said simply. "But we need more than proof. We need support. We're organizing a summit. Informal, for now. A gathering of those ready to reshape Tumblebrook's future without Monarch's shadow looming over it."

Ezra hesitated, the past flickering in his eyes. But then he gave a small, solemn nod—the kind of nod that carried decades of watching, waiting, and finally choosing to step into the light.

They reached out to Mr. Lark from Gossamer Fables, whose encyclopedic memory and extensive archive filled in many of the blanks Tobias had left behind. Eleanor Vance, the former school teacher whose dismissal years ago had been quietly orchestrated by Monarch sympathizers, arrived with boxes of lesson plans she'd never been permitted to teach—curricula that told the fuller, messier truth of Tumblebrook's past. Even shy young Nathaniel Harrow, usually reserved and solitary, stepped forward with a notarized letter that revealed his grandmother's land had been claimed illegally and then sold to a Monarch trustee. His voice trembled, but his resolve held.

Word spread faster than they expected. A widow who once served on the town's welcome committee offered her husband's journals, which chronicled strange discrepancies in council meetings. A grocer donated a hidden ledger, filled with transactions masked as donations. Each new voice was another crack in the wall Monarch had built.

They gathered that evening in the inn's garden room, surrounded by candles, notebooks, artifacts, and trembling resolve. The walls, lined with aged ivy and the comforting scent of rosemary and tea, became witness to a night of reckoning. Clara opened the meeting with a presentation of the timeline—projecting it on a makeshift screen, stringing together names, events, and the slow corruption that had grown in silence. Amelia followed with a call to vision: a future where no family was erased, no voice silenced for the convenience of a powerful few.

"We are not here to tear Tumblebrook apart," Amelia said, voice ringing with conviction. "We are here to replant it, to let it grow freely, wild if it must, but never again pruned into submission. This is our chance to grow it back, branch by branch, together."

There were nods, some tentative, others fervent. But not everyone in the room welcomed change.

From the back emerged a murmured warning. Alden Pike, a

retired council member and one-time Monarch sympathizer, raised a trembling voice. His face was drawn, but his eyes remained sharp.

"You must understand," he said, standing slowly, "Monarch protected more than it silenced. It gave order. Without it, who's to say chaos won't rush in? Families protected, businesses secured—it wasn't all control. Sometimes it was shelter."

Amelia met his eyes without flinching. "And who decided who deserved that shelter? Who chose who got erased to make room?"

He opened his mouth, then closed it, finally nodding in reluctant concession.

What followed were hours of tense discussion. Unexpected revelations sparked tears. Impassioned arguments fractured silence. There were disagreements—on how to approach reparations, how to document what was found, how to prepare for those who might resist with more than just words. Clara suggested discreet town hall-style forums. Ezra proposed a series of visual exhibitions—an art installation that would travel from shop to shop, unveiling the truth in images before words even had to be spoken.

Eleanor pushed for the restoration of the school's historical archives, long purged of uncomfortable truths. Nathaniel offered to create a digital repository—a living archive that could be updated by the community, not hidden by it. Amelia proposed a rotating council, one where every family in Tumblebrook could have a voice over time, ending the legacy of generational gatekeeping.

They began mapping their strategy for long-term protection. Clara volunteered to reach out to academic contacts to help oversee the archival process. Mr. Lark offered Gossamer Fables as a safe space for town meetings. A retired judge suggested creating a neutral committee to evaluate the misuse of power without igniting retribution.

Even amidst the dissent, there was momentum. By night's end, they had a framework. The first of many. But momentum was a fragile thing, and trust even more so. They knew the counterforce would rise. Monarch was a dragon with many heads, and though its breath may have cooled, its claws still scratched beneath the surface.

As the last lanterns dimmed and the participants filtered out, Amelia felt the weight of both hope and responsibility. She walked the inn's halls in silence, touching the banisters, the windowpanes, the framed portraits of past visitors. The building felt different now—less like a haven and more like a fulcrum. Everything pivoted here. It wasn't just history they were unearthing. It was the foundation for what came next.

The next morning brought wind and low gray skies. Amelia descended the staircase to find Lady Grey pacing by the door. Slipped through the mail slot was a sealed envelope.

The crest was unmistakable—three interlocked crowns in red ink. Not the Monarch butterfly—but something older, deeper. A symbol of authority cloaked in civility.

Amelia's hand shook slightly as she picked it up. Clara emerged from the dining room, watching silently as Amelia broke the seal.

Inside was a summons. She had been invited—no, requested—to appear before a newly reconstituted Monarch council. The location was unfamiliar, a private estate outside town limits. The time: dusk. The letter bore a single line beneath the address:

"We have heard you. Now you will hear us."

Lady Grey let out a long, low meow, circling Amelia's ankles once more.

Chapter 27

Monarch Disbanded

Clara Henderson adjusted the collar of her coat as she stepped onto the pebbled path leading to the remote estate where the reconstituted Monarch council had summoned Amelia. The morning fog hung low, curling like misted breath along the tree-lined road. The building ahead rose from it like a sentinel from another age—stoic, unwelcoming, and strangely fragile beneath its grandeur. The estate's ivy-covered stones whispered of secrets long kept, and Clara felt their weight as tangibly as the folio under her arm. Every step toward the estate echoed louder in her ears, reminding her she was not just a witness anymore—she was a messenger of reckoning.

Beside her, Amelia walked in silence. Her jaw was clenched, hands balled into steady fists inside her gloves, and her eyes sharp with quiet resolve. The silence between them wasn't one of unease, but of shared intention. The long and winding road that had brought them here—the scattered clues, buried histories, whispered confessions—had reached its terminus. The truth was no longer a question. It was a choice: to face it or bury it again. Their bond, forged in investigation and sleepless nights, pulsed like an unspoken vow.

Clara carried the final folio—a thick binder overflowing with annotated maps, testimony transcripts, Ezra's sketches, manipulated land deeds, and the remnants of Tobias Greer's journal. It was a weapon—not of violence, but of illumination. Tobias's handwriting still haunted her, a reminder that truth often came at a price.

Inside, the estate's great hall was dimly lit and rigidly formal. Candlelight flickered against tall windows. Seven chairs stood in a semicircle at the head of the chamber, each occupied by a senior member of Monarch. Their expressions were guarded, but Clara saw something deeper—weariness, uncertainty, perhaps even fear. Though the faces had changed, the tradition they upheld was centuries old.

Clara and Amelia stood without trembling.

Clara was the first to speak. "We are not here to threaten," she began, voice steady. "We are here to reveal. And we expect you to listen."

The council remained silent, but she sensed a shift. Readiness, or resignation. She placed the folio on the mahogany table, unfastened the clasp, and began.

They presented their findings: Ezra's sketches of secret meetings beneath town landmarks, Tobias's diary of eroded autonomy, land acquisitions favoring Monarch affiliates, testimonies of redirected lives. Page by page, the legacy of Monarch cracked like ice beneath heavy boots. Ignorance could no longer be claimed. Innocence no longer feigned.

The room, tense with defiance, shifted into silence. Clara watched them flinch at names, at signatures too old to contest, too clear to ignore. A councilman's hand trembled. Another removed glasses to rub his temples. Generations of weight bore down.

Amelia stepped forward, laying down Tobias's last letter, penned days before his disappearance.

"He wanted Tumblebrook to be free," she said, voice steady. "Not shackled to secrecy, but rooted in shared truth. This is not a crusade. It's a reckoning."

A long pause. Then the eldest—a woman with silver hair braided tight—stood. Her voice was quiet.

"Then it ends now. This legacy is not ours to pass down again."

One by one, the others rose. A small gesture, but one that carried the weight of generations. They did not speak, but their eyes met Clara's. Some tearful. Some humbled. None turned away.

Monarch disbanded not with fire, but with stillness. With accountability.

A motion to dissolve was passed. Signed by all. A copy given to Clara.

By the time Clara and Amelia returned to the inn, change was already rippling. Monarch symbols quietly disappeared from buildings. Long-silenced voices now spoke freely. Mr. Lark hosted public readings of censored histories. Eleanor Vance dusted off her lesson plans.

Town squares filled with conversation. Coffeehouses buzzed with ideas. The library received anonymous donations of long-lost records. A document titled The Tumblebrook Accord began circulating, codifying transparency, leadership equity, and memory protection.

Clara watched the transformation with cautious hope. The roots of Monarch were deep. But real change had begun. Young townsfolk stepped up. Inclusive committees formed. Murals replaced faded Monarch symbolism. One wall bore a quote from Tobias's journal: "No truth thrives in silence."

Speaking at Gossamer Fables, Clara held up the original folio. "Transparency is a choice. We choose it now. Not for spectacle, but for stewardship."

Applause followed—not of excitement, but of resolve. Clara felt it then: she had become more than a clerk. She was a keeper of memory. A restorer of balance.

The upcoming autumn festival was reimagined. No cloaked rites or whispered vows. It would celebrate resilience, creativity, and truth. Storytelling, art, lantern lighting. Children rehearsed dances. Bakers tested new recipes. Ezra unveiled a new series: What Was Hidden. A playwright penned a drama based on Tobias. A monument was proposed—not to Monarch, but to courage.

Even Lady Grey seemed freer, trailing festival planners like a queen at rest.

As Clara stood in the square, Lady Grey wound around her legs with a contented purr. Amelia joined her. Laughter rang out, hammers tapped, music drifted from a violinist nearby.

"Do you think it will last?" Clara asked.

Amelia's gaze swept the square. "Only shards of mystery remain. But this—this is hope. And hope, I think, is finally louder than fear."

Chapter 28

Festival of Light

Amelia Farnsworth stood beneath the arched wooden trellis that framed the entrance to Tumblebrook's central square, now adorned in warm lanterns and ribbons of deep burgundy and gold. Autumn had fully arrived, crisp air mingling with the scent of apple cider, roasted nuts, pine needles, cinnamon, and honeyed pastries wafting through the breeze. The Festival of Light was in full swing, and for the first time in years, Amelia felt no heaviness in her chest, no shadows to sidestep, no lingering weight from the secrets that once haunted the town like morning fog. Her eyes glistened—not from sorrow, but from something far rarer: peace.

The square buzzed with energy and warmth, its rhythm as steady as a heartbeat. Children twirled with hand-crafted paper lanterns painted with starlit skies and mythical creatures. Vendors called out specials from their booths, laughter rising and falling like waves. Strings of fairy lights crisscrossed above the cobblestone paths, casting a gentle glow that illuminated not just faces but spirits. Every smile felt sincere, every handshake genuine. This was a different kind of celebration—one not built on secrecy or tradition for tradition's sake, but on choice, on clarity, on connection.

Everywhere she looked, Amelia saw a town reinventing itself. Wooden signs bore the emblems of new collectives—artist guilds, historical cooperatives, garden shares—all springing from the ground like wildflowers in bloom. The former gloom of deference had been replaced with the sparkle of collaboration. Teenagers handed out flyers for their new community zine, The Tumbletruth. Grandmothers knitted scarves with interwoven stories, while younger parents organized storytime circles around bonfires. The town breathed in rhythm with its people.

The town had changed. Amelia could see it in the way people greeted one another, not with polite reservation, but with unguarded joy. Families who had once kept to themselves during Monarch's reign now mingled freely. Former skeptics joined hands with hopeful dreamers. People once opposed on principle now collaborated on building booths and planning the festival program. The festival had become a mirror of the new Tumblebrook—open, vibrant, and evolving.

Amelia wove through the crowd with practiced ease, greeting every familiar face. She stopped often to check on each stall, ensuring vendors had what they needed, that their displays glowed with warmth and intention. Her passion for hospitality had found new life in the freedom this season offered. Gone were the stiff, ceremonial traditions that clung to the past like ivy on stone. In their place heartfelt celebration bloomed. Her own booth—a pop-up from the Tumblebrook Inn—offered warm pumpkin scones drizzled with caramel glaze, steaming cups of cinnamon tea, and handwritten recipe cards lovingly prepared. Guests lingered not just for flavor, but for comfort, for story, for the kindness that emanated from her space.

"Amelia!" called Doris Finch, waving her over with flour-dusted fingers from behind a mountain of sugared doughnuts. Her cheeks were flushed from the heat of her fryer, her apron smudged with pride. "You've got to try this glaze—new recipe, straight from Eleanor's old book!"

Laughing, Amelia accepted a warm pastry and thanked her,

savoring both the treat and the woman's visible joy. The doughnut melted on her tongue with hints of orange and cardamom. There had been healing here, too. Doris, once known more for her gossip than her grace, had channeled her storytelling gift into a booth of her own, where townsfolk gathered nightly to hear legends, local histories, and tales once stifled by silence. She was, in her own way, rewriting the town's narrative.

Ezra's installation stood at the square's center—a spiraled sculpture of iron, copper, and driftwood, each layer inscribed with a phrase from Tobias's journal or a quote from the townspeople's oral histories. It pulsed with life, lit from within by gently flickering lanterns, and drew visitors like moths to firelight. Some stood silently before it, hands clasped in reverence. Others wept quietly, moved by the raw honesty of it. But most smiled—because what they saw reflected back at them was resilience.

At one point, the community broke into a spontaneous chorus led by the town's choir. Amelia joined in with laughter, linking arms with strangers and old friends alike. A group of children performed a lantern-lit puppet play based on a reimagined version of the town's founding—this time, including the silenced voices, the forgotten families, and the quiet rebels. It was whimsical, pointed, and healing all at once.

Amelia paused by Ezra's sculpture, fingers brushing the smooth wood where her own handwriting had joined the spiral: "We share the light. We do not own it." The words had come to her one morning at sunrise, and now they glowed with quiet meaning.

She was about to turn away when she noticed Ezra approaching from the other side of the sculpture, a wrapped bundle under one arm and Lady Grey trailing closely behind him, regal as ever.

"I thought you might want this," Ezra said, unwrapping a delicate wood carving. It was of Lady Grey, perched atop an open book, her tail curled around the spine like a comma of curiosity. On the book's pages were inscribed a familiar pattern—Tobias's final notes, now carved into permanence.

Amelia blinked, surprised. "Ezra, this is… it's beautiful."

"I made it for the archive room," he said with a modest shrug, his eyes crinkling. "But I think Lady Grey would prefer you have it. Besides, you're the keeper of the inn. Of our stories."

As if on cue, the silver-furred cat twitched her whiskers and turned, weaving her way through the legs of passersby, clearly intent on something. Amelia and Ezra exchanged a curious look.

"She's up to something," Amelia murmured.

Lady Grey padded past booths filled with candles, crafts, and memory jars. She passed under banners bearing words like integrity, healing, and legacy. She made a beeline across the square, unbothered by the crowd, until she reached the edge of the festivities, where the soft grass gave way to the mossy path leading toward the old bookshop.

Clara, already waiting outside with a tray of freshly steeped chai, raised an eyebrow as the cat approached and flicked her tail twice.

"She came from your direction," Clara said, handing Amelia a cup.

"She has a nose for history," Amelia replied, crouching beside her feline companion.

Lady Grey meowed softly, then slipped through the narrow space between the shop's side wall and the overgrown rose hedge. Amelia hesitated.

Ezra gestured to follow. "Maybe it's one of her hunches."

Together, the three humans and one determined cat made their way along the side path, leaves crunching softly beneath their boots. Lady Grey stopped before a bramble-covered wooden grate set low into the foundation. Ezra crouched and brushed the leaves aside.

"There's something here," he whispered.

He tugged at the grate. It came free with a rusty groan, revealing a short tunnel—cool, musty, and lined with old bricks. Lady Grey hopped in without a second thought.

"Guess we're going spelunking," Clara murmured.

With lanterns borrowed from nearby booths, they crawled inside.

The passage led to a forgotten basement chamber below the shop, filled with decaying wooden crates, rolled parchments, brittle leather-bound volumes, and faded documents marked with outdated seals. Dust danced in the lantern light like suspended stars. In one corner, protected by an oilskin satchel, was a stack of sealed letters and a locked box adorned with the Monarch crest—crossed out in red ink.

Amelia exhaled slowly. "He left this for us."

There was reverence in the silence that followed. Clara reached out, brushing dust from the nearest letter. The name on the envelope had been smudged by time, but Amelia recognized the handwriting.

"It's Tobias," she said softly. "His final chapter."

Chapter 29

Altering Opportunities

Clara stood at the front of Gossamer Fables, the beloved bookshop filled with guests on this golden-hued autumn morning. The space had been transformed for the day's special purpose. Normally a cozy labyrinth of tall wooden shelves and hidden nooks, the shop had been carefully rearranged to host a historic auction. Ivy-laced garlands adorned the doorframes, and framed sketches of the old town lined the back wall beside candlelit tables bearing aged artifacts. Today's gathering wasn't just about raising funds—it was about acknowledging the past, releasing it with intention, and repurposing its meaning for a brighter future.

Tables lined with relics once hidden away in vaults and private safes now shimmered under the filtered sunlight that poured through the bookshop's grand windows. There were candlestick holders engraved with Monarch's sigil, journals half-erased by time and scribbled margins, pieces of heirloom lace and silver spoons recovered from attics and cellars, some still wrapped in yellowed newspaper. Objects that had once symbolized silence and control were now labeled with stories of resilience. Clara had curated each item meticulously, pairing them with hand-lettered placards that told their origin stories—but more importantly, reclaimed their narratives. These items were no longer icons of power. They were conversation pieces. Artifacts of recovery.

She adjusted the lapel of her corduroy jacket and took a breath. Her fingers trembled slightly—not from nerves, but from the weight of the day. She wasn't just auctioning antiques; she was guiding a community toward healing. Each object was a seed, capable of planting understanding, if nurtured correctly. Nearby, a handwritten banner reading "From Shadows to Light" hung from a windowpane, catching the sunlight just so. Clara had hung it herself at dawn.

"Good morning, everyone," Clara began, her voice calm yet steady, echoing softly through the hushed room. "Today isn't about preserving Monarch's memory. It's about transforming what once was. These pieces will not return to the shadows. They will live among us—in light, in learning, and in the commitment to do better."

The crowd, a blend of townsfolk both old and young, nodded. Some clutched bidding paddles. Others simply came to observe. Teachers, artists, librarians, bakers, farmers—they filled the room with curiosity and a kind of sacred attentiveness. The energy wasn't solemn, but reverent. A few even dabbed at tears as Clara moved from one artifact to the next, telling short stories of recovered truth and shared courage.

The auction began.

Some items drew quick bids. A hand-etched decanter set fetched an early offer from the new owner of the café, who planned to display it as part of a historical tasting nook. A series of Monarch correspondence letters—now separated from their oppressive context—were claimed by the local museum. Other pieces were met with more subdued interest, taken home by residents who saw meaning in their imperfections. A cracked mirror that once hung in the Monarch hall was purchased by a sculptor planning to refashion it into a mosaic.

Children helped pass the items in boxes lined with velvet. Every detail had been considered: reused paper for the auction sheets, compostable cups of cider and tea served by the inn's kitchen, and even a gratitude board near the entrance, where people could write messages or draw memories. Clara spotted messages like, "To my grandmother, who taught me truth matters," and "Here's to beginning again."

Clara noticed how easily people leaned into one another, murmuring questions, sharing insights. An older man whose family had suffered under Monarch's rule exchanged words—and a warm smile—with a young woman whose grandfather had once sat on the secret council. The air was no longer charged with suspicion. It was filled with a cautious optimism, the fragile trust of a town rediscovering itself. For the first time, they were not just confronting the past—they were accepting it, together.

Healing, Clara thought, wasn't always loud. Sometimes it came in the quiet shuffle of feet as people browsed records without fear. Sometimes it arrived in the way one person helped another lift a heavy box, or when a child asked what the symbol on a plaque meant, and an adult answered honestly. She saw it in the clasped hands of two neighbors long estranged, sharing a laugh about an artifact they'd both remembered from childhood.

When the final item—a carved wooden box inlaid with fragments of the original town charter—was claimed by the local school for a public heritage exhibit, Clara felt something internal unlock. This was what altering opportunities looked like. Not erasing history, but transforming it. Not forgetting, but choosing to remember in the light.

After the auction, Clara stepped outside and inhaled deeply. The festival continued down the main road, vibrant and alive. Music from a string quartet drifted on the breeze, accompanied by the soft thud of children's feet playing hopscotch on chalk-drawn constellations. The lanterns swayed above the streets like stars brought down to earth, and every corner of the town seemed to glow. A sense of balance settled into the bricks beneath her feet.

Adaptive change was everywhere. Ezra had started an art program in the park called "Lines of Legacy," pairing teenagers with retirees to sketch and share life stories. Amelia had expanded her community nights at the inn to include open-hearth dinners, where locals brought recipes passed down through generations and shared them with stories and laughter. Mr. Lark had transformed the entire back wing of the bookstore into a research room dubbed "Truths Reclaimed," where townspeople were encouraged to leave stories, letters, and reflections. Even the high school began planning a civic history curriculum.

Even the smallest acts were meaningful. A young girl helped repaint the mural on the old train depot, adding Monarch's fallen crest split by a sunrise. An elderly couple organized an afternoon tea dedicated to forgotten voices in the town's archives. A local choir reworked an old Monarch hymn into a ballad of rebirth and unity. Fear no longer dictated interaction. Curiosity, creativity, and connection had taken its place.

That evening, under the warm glow of the festival lanterns, Clara gathered with Amelia, Ezra, Doris, Mr. Lark, and dozens of other townsfolk on the lawn outside the inn. Folding chairs formed a circle, cider passed from hand to hand. They told stories—not with bitterness, but with clarity. Not as a way to judge, but to teach, to reflect. Generations sat side by side, weaving threads of memory and hope.

Then came the moment Clara hadn't anticipated.

A town elder—Mrs. Corwin, one of the longest-standing historians in Tumblebrook—approached the circle, her cane tapping lightly over the cobblestones. In her other hand she held a brass key and a leather-bound volume. Her voice, when she spoke, was resolute.

"We think it's time these were no longer buried," she said, offering them to Clara.

Inside the book were outlines—not just of Monarch's structure, but of alternative systems proposed by those who had questioned it in quiet over the decades. Models for shared governance. Collaborative leadership. Distributed accountability. These were not dreams, but blueprints—refined, tested, and preserved by citizens who had hoped one day to pass them forward.

As Clara flipped through the pages, a hush fell again. It was not silence of fear, but of awakening. The crowd leaned closer. Even the children grew still.

"These aren't just ideas," she said. "They're opportunities. A foundation we can choose to build from."

The crowd murmured its agreement, growing louder with affirmation. And as they did, Clara could feel it: the fear that once shrouded governance dissolving, replaced by determination. By trust. By collective courage.

Chapter 30

Scholarly Pursuits

Amelia Farnsworth stood before the arched threshold of Tumblebrook's newly renovated Hall of Learning, a structure that had once served as the exclusive enclave for Monarch's archival society. For decades, it had loomed as an impenetrable place, cloaked in elitism and sealed with selective knowledge. Now, its ivy-covered exterior shimmered with purpose anew—banners of sunflowers, owls, and open books fluttered from its eaves, and wide glass windows welcomed the light. For the first time in its long history, it felt like a place not of division, but of invitation.

Inside, the main atrium buzzed with quiet industry. Long tables were arranged with notebooks, sketchpads, magnifying glasses, and artifacts awaiting cataloging. Youthful voices whispered among shelves stocked with fresh materials, while older mentors leaned in, guiding them with the gentleness of shared healing. The scent of aged parchment blended with brewed coffee and the faint trace of beeswax candles. Soft piano music played from a corner radio—an old recording of a local composer Clara had unearthed from the town's forgotten archives. Everything inside hummed with new life.

Amelia had been invited to speak that morning at a symposium on community archives and evolving narratives. The idea of giving a formal talk had once terrified her. She was a woman of routines, someone who had spent years polishing banisters and folding linens with crisp precision. Yet now, she found her voice with the ease of someone who had lived through transformation and grown stronger for it. She stood at the front of the atrium, palms resting on a wooden podium carved with the town's new emblem—an open lantern flanked by quills—and waited for the hush to settle.

"This town's story is no longer a secret," she began, her voice firm but warm. "And the value of our past lies not in who controlled it, but in how we've chosen to share it—with each other, and with those yet to come."

A ripple of affirmation moved through the room. Ezra, seated in the third row with a sketchbook in his lap, offered a quiet, proud smile. Clara—flanked by three teen researchers in matching wool scarves—nodded with quiet intensity. Mr. Lark, ever the bookshop sage, leaned forward with hands clasped, as if absorbing every syllable.

In recent weeks, an unanticipated wave of academic and cultural enthusiasm had surged through Tumblebrook. The town's curiosity had ignited a movement. Libraries reopened with expanded sections dedicated to oral histories and handwritten memoirs. Park workshops taught everything from folklore interpretation to ancestral baking techniques. Schools introduced independent study programs where students interviewed elders, digitized journals, and curated micro-exhibits.

What had begun as a search for truth amidst Monarch's ruins had become something greater—a shared hunger to unearth every layer of their collective heritage. Residents who once assumed their stories didn't matter found themselves invited to panels. The young, once disengaged, arrived early at the Hall's reading room, hands ink-stained and eyes bright with discovery.

Even outsiders had taken notice. Professors from Twin Harbors University offered collaboration, citing Tumblebrook as a model for grassroots archival reformation. Filmmakers requested to document restoration projects. State archivists visited to advise on cataloging practices. The inn's mail slot brimmed with letters from distant relatives and curious scholars, eager to be part of the town's reawakening.

Amelia, both proud and humbled, found herself unexpectedly at the center. She received invitations to moderate forums on community stewardship, helped organize readings of Tobias's essays, and even contributed to drafting a new civic mission statement. It was more than she ever imagined—and yet, it fit.

One golden afternoon, as sun filtered through the Hall's stained-glass windows, Amelia strolled through the reading garden with two students: Ava, a bookish girl drawn to archival science, and Marcus, a soft-spoken storyteller fascinated by local myths. They pointed out etchings carved into stones—remnants of a time when Monarch had left its symbols in plain sight.

"Do you think Monarch had more sites?" Marcus asked, flipping through his sketchbook.

"Possibly," Amelia replied. "But what matters more is that you're the ones asking now. You're following trails we never dared to explore."

Ava looked up. "It's like we've inherited a mystery. But instead of fear, we're approaching it with wonder."

That sentiment became a quiet mantra.

Newsletters began publishing weekly "Then & Now" columns highlighting cultural shifts. A new community journal—The Lantern Review—launched under Clara's guidance, brimming with essays, interviews, and poetry. Debates over truth preservation and shared memory became a regular feature at the café and the inn's long tables.

The peak of this collaboration came during a mentorship dinner on the inn's back lawn, beneath a canopy of fairy lights. Each seat bore a notecard with the name of a resident affected by Monarch's reign—some victims, some complicit, all now part of the story. Platters of food passed freely. Conversations flowed. A former Monarch member shared tea with a young activist. Their words were candid.

"It's humbling," the elder said. "To realize the truths we ignored."

"And brave," the youth replied, "to admit it now."

Amelia felt tears rise. This—this was what she had hoped for. Not performance, but participation. Not perfection, but progress. Purposeful engagement now rooted deep in the town's soil, growing into something rare: a hunger not for prestige, but for wisdom. For connection.

And just when she thought they had reached a kind of calm completeness, another mystery arrived.

It came in the form of an envelope, slipped beneath the inn's kitchen door late one night. No return address. Only a single symbol: a crescent moon cradled within a compass rose. Inside, on pristine parchment, a message in elegant script:

To forget is to risk repeating. But not all has yet been remembered. There are layers still below.

Amelia reread the note by lamplight, heart quickening. It wasn't a threat, nor comfort. It felt familiar—like a whisper from an unfinished chapter.

She turned to Lady Grey, perched near the window, tail curled, gaze steady.

Amelia placed the letter beside the ledger of Tobias's final writings.

The past, it seemed, was not finished with them yet.

Chapter 31

Lady Grey's Curiosity

Clara had grown used to Lady Grey's peculiar behavior. Over the past few months, the feline had become something of a local legend in her own right—Tumblebrook's resident oracle, silent sage, and mischief-maker wrapped in a velvety silver coat. Where she wandered, clues often followed. Her knack for appearing precisely where she was needed had transcended coincidence. Now, whenever Clara saw the cat pause and fix her wide, intelligent eyes on a spot for too long, she knew better than to dismiss it.

This morning, the pair of them were tucked into the sunlit nook of Gossamer Fables' reading loft. Lady Grey rested on the windowsill, tail twitching thoughtfully as she surveyed the activity outside. Clara, notebook in hand, had been jotting down notes from the latest batch of letters discovered in the archive's northern wing. The scent of warm croissants wafted up from the café below, mingling with the mellow sound of a cello recording that played softly on the phonograph. The light filtered through stained-glass panels in soft ribbons, casting color across the floorboards and bringing a reverent hush to the usually bustling loft.

But Lady Grey wasn't interested in music or breakfast. Her attention had locked onto a thin beam of sunlight that illuminated the far end of the top bookshelf—a dusty alcove most had ignored for years. Clara followed her gaze, noticing for the first time how the light perfectly framed a worn stretch of binding and an indentation in the wooden paneling.

"You've got something on your mind, haven't you?" Clara said, rising from her seat. The cat let out a single, decisive chirrup and flicked her tail.

Clara climbed the narrow ladder affixed to the bookshelf and reached behind a row of outdated tax records. Her fingers brushed against something cold.

A tin box.

It was heavier than expected. Carefully, she pulled it free and carried it down to the rug. Inside were tightly rolled scrolls of parchment bound with string, an envelope bearing a wax seal in the shape of a rose, and a brass pendant etched with unfamiliar markings. Lady Grey followed her down and sat beside her, curling neatly into a watchful ball.

The documents detailed early visions from the dissenting members of Monarch—philosophers, artists, and historians who had once tried to steer the group toward transparency and inclusivity before being silenced or ignored. Their writings were poetic, filled with questions rather than commands. One scroll began, *"What is a town if not the reflection of its shared longing?"* Another quoted an unknown thinker: *"To preserve truth, one must first allow it to breathe."*

Clara's heart stirred. These weren't just counter-narratives—they were a framework. A reminder that even in the heart of deception, there had been those who dared to envision better. The contents weren't just historical—they were aspirational. Their words felt like breadcrumbs leading forward, not just echoes of the past.

The pendant, when turned over, bore a series of coordinates and the inscription: *To those who still seek, walk the spiral and listen.* Clara's pulse quickened.

Downstairs, she shared the find with Amelia and Ezra. They spread the contents across the inn's long kitchen table. By midday, a small crowd had gathered. The scrolls, Tobias's journal entries, and the recently uncovered ledger now formed a trifecta of knowledge that offered depth and dimension to Tumblebrook's evolving truth.

Lady Grey prowled the perimeter of the gathering, occasionally hopping onto the table to point her nose at a passage or paw at a scroll, much to the amusement—and now reverence—of those present. The cat had become something more than a companion. She was a curator, a quiet catalyst. Even the children treated her with solemnity, calling her *"Professor Grey"* in hushed, admiring tones.

What unfolded over the next few days was nothing short of astonishing.

Tumblebrook found itself galvanized once more, not by fear or secrecy, but by curiosity and shared purpose. Residents volunteered to catalog what Clara jokingly dubbed *"Lady Grey's Archive."* Teenagers with smartphones and scanning apps worked side-by-side with octogenarians holding magnifying glasses. Elders began sharing long-forgotten family legends. Teachers developed new elective courses inspired by the writings. Children reenacted discovery scenes at the festival's storytelling hour, acting out Lady Grey's intuition like a furry detective hero complete with cloaks, monocles, and tiny notebooks.

The scrolls were exhibited in a rotating display at the Hall of Learning. One evening, as lanterns glowed gently along the walkways and live folk music played nearby, Clara hosted a reading session beneath the stars. She watched as young adults debated the ethics raised in one parchment while an elderly couple held hands nearby, reflecting on how the town had changed. Ezra read aloud from a scroll by lantern light, his voice crackling with emotion as he recited a passage about communal responsibility and legacy.

Clara, watching it all unfold, felt something expand inside her.

She thought back to how hesitant she'd once been—to get involved, to believe, to lead. But now she saw her role differently. Not as a bystander, but a bridge. A conduit between insight and action. It was never about being the loudest voice in the room, but about asking the right questions and encouraging others to seek their own answers.

Lady Grey's presence served as a balm for doubt and as a spark for inspiration. When Clara felt overwhelmed by the sheer weight of all they were uncovering, the cat would appear—settling into her lap or nudging her toward the next mystery. The townspeople had started calling her an honorary librarian. A small plaque had even been placed in her favorite sunlit nook: *"Reserved for Lady Grey: Guardian of Wisdom."*

During one particularly lively evening discussion at the inn, Clara posed a question to the room: "What if everything we need to build a better future is already here—hidden in the spaces we walk past every day?"

No one laughed. No one rolled their eyes. They just nodded. The silence that followed wasn't awkward—it was contemplative. A collective breath of agreement.

That night, Clara wrote in her journal: Lady Grey reminds us that curiosity is its own kind of courage. That peace isn't born from silence, but from listening to the questions no one else has thought to ask. That inspiration lives in the quiet, in the corners, in the overlooked, and the persistent. She leads without demand, and in her stillness, she teaches us how to look again.

A few days later, a group of students proposed a community time capsule. Everyone contributed something—quotes, drawings, small items that represented their hopes or learnings. Clara, inspired by Lady Grey's example, contributed a tiny silver bell with the inscription: *"For those who follow the whisper."* The capsule was buried in the courtyard beneath the magnolia tree, its coordinates etched into a commemorative plaque that read, *"Unlocked by those brave enough to question."*

In the months that followed, Tumblebrook continued to flourish

—not with fanfare or grand declarations, but with quiet, determined steps. Book clubs, mentorship circles, storytelling festivals, and educational pilgrimages all drew from the wellspring of what Lady Grey had uncovered. Clara watched as the next generation embraced the pursuit not just of answers, but of meaning.

Chapter 32

A Journey Begins

Amelia Farnsworth stood at the edge of the Tumblebrook Inn's wraparound porch, her hands cradling a warm mug of chamomile tea. The sun had just begun to rise over the hills, casting golden hues across the mist-draped rooftops of the town. From this vantage, she could see the steeple of the Hall of Learning, the winding trails of the central garden, and the tall, slender chimney of Gossamer Fables gently exhaling a curl of smoke. Everything looked calm, purposeful, and alive.

She took a sip of her tea and breathed deeply, allowing the scent of lavender and fresh pine to fill her lungs. This quiet, reflective moment had become her new morning ritual. The peace was well-earned. The world she knew had changed—but not in ways that demanded fear. Instead, the changes had felt like the slow blooming of a field after winter. Subtle, beautiful, and entirely necessary.

Transformation had been the word on everyone's lips for weeks now—transformation of tradition, of space, of hearts. But for Amelia, it had been more than that. It had been a journey back into herself, one shaped not only by the unraveling of Monarch's legacy but by the blossoming of a new, collective spirit within Tumblebrook. What had started as an investigation into a missing man had turned into a reckoning with the town's past and a reaffirmation of its future.

As she moved to settle into the porch rocker, the door creaked open behind her.

"Morning," Clara greeted, carrying a stack of journals and a croissant she had clearly pilfered from the inn kitchen.

"Good morning," Amelia replied with a smile. "You're up early again."

"Cataloging Lady Grey's Archives," Clara said, dropping the books onto the table beside them. "And double-checking the transcriptions from the Rose Seal scrolls. You know how Mr. Lark is about accuracy."

Amelia chuckled softly. "We've all become scholars."

Clara leaned against the railing, eyes scanning the horizon. "We've become believers. In truth. In each other."

Amelia nodded, moved by how much those words resonated. They had fought for light and brought it forward—not by force, but by invitation. By listening. By letting go.

The sound of soft paws interrupted the stillness. Lady Grey emerged from the doorway, her silver coat catching the dawn's glow like moonlight. She blinked up at both women, tail high, before leaping gracefully onto the railing beside Clara and curling herself into a regal loaf.

"She approves," Clara said with a grin.

"She always knows," Amelia added. "I've started to think she understands more about this town than any of us."

From the hill, bells chimed. A new day had officially begun, and with it came a renewed energy that pulsed through the cobbled streets and rose-colored buildings. Children played near the inn's gate, skipping rope and shouting lines from stories they'd read in the town's new journal. Shopkeepers opened shutters with bright faces. The baker waved from across the square. The ripple of community moved like wind through trees—soft, unstoppable.

The legacy of Monarch no longer loomed. Instead, it whispered—a reminder of what had been, a compass pointing toward what should never be repeated. In its place had grown something resilient and radiant: a community that valued story over secrecy, discovery over dominance.

A week earlier, a town meeting had been held in the open-air amphitheater, where every seat was filled and standing room overflowed. A new charter was read aloud—one formed by collective voice, debated and refined with care. Its language championed transparency, equity, stewardship, and kindness. The vote to ratify had been unanimous.

Ezra, now affectionately known as the Town Archivist, had painted a mural along the outer wall of the amphitheater—a depiction of Lady Grey standing on a bookshelf, surrounded by stars and open books, watching over the town below. Children would often stop and pet the wall, giggling as if the painted cat might purr.

"I think she's a bit smug about it," Clara said as she watched Lady Grey stretch luxuriously.

"She earned it," Amelia replied.

Since the final revelations about Monarch, the inn had become more than a place to sleep—it was now a hub of ideas and healing. Artists sketched beneath the pergola, historians held quiet interviews in the solarium, and storytellers recited local lore in the parlor where Tobias's voice once echoed. Even strangers who passed through left with more than souvenirs—they took with them the spirit of a town rediscovered.

At that moment, as if summoned by some invisible rhythm, Mr. Lark arrived at the gate with the morning mail. "Special delivery!" he called, waving a thick, cream-colored envelope in the air.

Amelia took it with curiosity. The front bore her name in looping script. No return address.

She opened it, and her breath caught.

Inside was a short note:

"Some truths end chapters. Others begin them. There's more to the

map than we've seen. Look beyond the lake, where old stones sleep. - A Friend"

Beneath the message was a sketch of what looked like a broken compass, with a new direction drawn where north used to be.

Clara read over her shoulder. "Do you think...?"

Amelia smiled slowly. "I think the story isn't over."

Lady Grey purred deeply and rose to her feet, her tail curling in anticipation. Her eyes sparkled, as if she too sensed what was coming.

The sun climbed higher, illuminating every corner of Tumblebrook—its paths and porches, its towers and taverns, its fields and faces. Hope gleamed like dew on grass. The town was no longer hiding. It was opening. Embracing. Preparing.

A new festival had been announced—*The Lantern of Legacy Celebration*. It would celebrate not only the town's past but also its promise. Each participant would carry a hand-decorated lantern to the lake's edge, letting the light float across the water as a symbol of what they had let go, and what they were ready to pursue. Amelia had chosen hers already—glass etched with winding ivy and a carved silhouette of a cat atop an open book.

Amelia looked at Clara, then at Lady Grey.

"Shall we?" she asked.

Lady Grey leapt off the railing and trotted toward the path.

Clara adjusted her satchel, filled not with tools of investigation now, but journals, maps, and fresh ink.

And Amelia—heart full, eyes bright—stepped forward.

The journey had never truly ended. It had simply begun again.

Epilogue

The Lightkeeper's Ledger

The lake was still.

Its surface mirrored the moonlight with such precision that it looked like a second sky—one where stars floated instead of burned. Lanterns bobbed gently across the water, each a glowing tribute, carrying words, wishes, and memories written by hand and heart. Tumblebrook's Lantern of Legacy Celebration had begun, and with it, a new tradition—one not drawn from secrecy or shadow, but from story.

Amelia Farnsworth stood barefoot at the lake's edge, her lantern cradled in her hands. Etched with ivy and the silhouette of a cat perched atop an open book, it felt less like a tribute and more like a promise. The cool breeze whispered through the birch trees. Behind her, townspeople murmured softly, sending off their own lights—each one a chapter, a lesson, a letting-go.

She turned slightly as Clara approached, her lantern glowing gold with copper filigree. On one side, she had written a line from Tobias's journal: *"Truth may sleep, but it dreams of being found."*

"It's beautiful," Amelia said, voice hushed.

"So is yours." Clara smiled, nudging shoulders with her. "Are you ready?"

Amelia glanced down at the lantern one more time, then nodded. "I think I've been ready longer than I knew."

They stepped forward in unison, releasing their lanterns into the water. The lights joined dozens of others, drifting slowly outward in shimmering procession. Some bore drawings. Others, poetry. One child's lantern simply read: *For tomorrow.*

At the base of the dock, Lady Grey sat like a statue, tail curled neatly around her paws. Her amber eyes never left the horizon. She blinked once—slowly, wisely—as if she too understood the weight of the moment.

The crowd stood in collective silence, breath held as their lights became constellations.

Ezra's voice broke the hush. He stood farther up the shoreline with a sketchpad in hand, capturing the scene in charcoal strokes. "They look like dreams floating free," he said.

"Maybe they are," said Mr. Lark, his gaze faraway. "Maybe this is how history should always be carried—not locked in vaults, but lit and shared."

Soft applause followed. The townspeople lingered, unwilling to leave the moment just yet. They spoke in gentle tones. Shared cider. Sang songs too old to trace. For one night, time didn't press forward. It simply held them—together.

Later, as the crowd dispersed and the lanterns drifted out of sight, Clara and Amelia walked the shoreline one last time. Lady Grey padded ahead of them, tail swaying like a metronome set to the rhythm of change.

"I've been thinking," Clara said quietly, "we should publish it."

Amelia raised an eyebrow. "Publish what?"

"Everything. Not just Tobias's notes, not just Monarch's history. *Our* version. The whole journey. From the inn to the ruins. From secrecy to sunlight."

Amelia considered it. "A ledger of light," she murmured.

Clara smiled. "Exactly."

Amelia tilted her head. "Do we include Lady Grey as co-author?"

"I was thinking *editor-in-chief,*" Clara said.

A laugh escaped them both, light and free. In the hush that followed, they stood watching the last lantern disappear into the dark, its glow still visible—a tiny beacon of what had been and what could still be.

And in that moment, the past no longer felt like a burden.

It felt like a map.

A story.

A beginning.